T0147038

Broken
2

Broken
2

THE FIX

CAITLIN LINDULA

BROKEN 2
THE FIX

iUniverse books may be ordered through booksellers or by contacting:

iUniverse
1663 Liberty Drive
Bloomington, IN 47403
www.iuniverse.com
1-800-Authors (1-800-288-4677)

Because of the dynamic nature of the Internet, any web addresses or links contained in this book may have changed since publication and may no longer be valid. The views expressed in this work are solely those of the author and do not necessarily reflect the views of the publisher, and the publisher hereby disclaims any responsibility for them.

The views expressed in this work are solely those of the author
and do not necessarily reflect the views of the publisher, and the
publisher hereby disclaims any responsibility for them.

Any people depicted in stock imagery provided by Getty Images are models,
and such images are being used for illustrative purposes only.
Certain stock imagery © Getty Images.

ISBN: 978-1-5320-7265-9 (sc)
ISBN: 978-1-5320-7266-6 (e)

Print information available on the last page.

iUniverse rev. date: 04/02/2019

Chapter 1

After Midnight had opened the door with shock asking why Harmony was there, Harmony was finally able to speak, "I came back because I felt bad about not telling you how and why I knew about what had happened to your mother. Not only that but what could happen to you as well, may I come in and explain myself?" Midnight thought for a moment then nodded and stepped back while opening the door wider for her to come in.

Harmony sat down while Midnight was getting her a glass of blood, when Midnight sat down Harmony took a deep breath and let it out. She took a sip of her drink the spoke, "the reason I didn't tell you is because I had seen it long before Mary could. If I were to have told you or your mother, I would have risked one or both of you running to her asking if it's the truth. She would have looked at the test results from your mother's blood samples again, in shock and ask how you knew.

I didn't want the whole neighborhood knowing that I can see the future now not only for myself but for others as well, only when it's going to end badly though." Midnight just sat there in shock for a moment, she opened her mouth to get ready to say something. Harmony cut her off, "that and I needed you to say it out loud to yourself, so you actually realize what's going on. Before I could come back, I then realized you were going to need my help.

What I want you to do now is come with me outside, so I can hear you verbally say what's happened, not just mentally." Midnight stood up, but she didn't move after that for a few minutes, so Harmony had to grab her hand and guide her to the door. When they got outside Harmony and her sit on the chair that was there, so she wouldn't collapse to the ground when saying it. Midnight took a deep breath, let it out and at first quietly said, "my mother has a big possibility that she could not only change back to human, but she could die while it happens."

Midnight went quiet after that, Harmony spoke, "I didn't hear you, you need to say it louder." Just to try to shut her up, Midnight spoke so she could hear it, "my mother has a big possibility that she could not only change back into a human, but she could die while it happens." Harmony spoke again, "good now you need to say what's going to happen to her if they can't stop it and if they can." Midnight lifted her head up and gave the look of "I might kill you after we are done here", but instead of saying that she just closed her eyes took another deep breath and spoke, "if they can't stop it, she is going to die".

"And…." Harmony said, "if they can?" Midnight spoke quickly, "if they can, she still might die, but if she doesn't she won't be her normal self. There I said it are you happy now?!" Midnight ended up shouting and crying the last part, when she was finished with shouting she was crying hard into Harmony's shoulder. Harmony awkwardly patted her on the back and asked why she was crying so hard, Midnight replied with, "because I'm scared it's going to happen to me."

She continued to cry, until she fell asleep and Harmony had to carry her to her room. Harmony covered her up with the blanket, kissed Midnight's forehead, took a step back and whispered, "I am sorry for what I am about to do. It will be a lot better for the both of us just trust me, I can't say that because you won't even remember me." With one wave of her hand over Midnight's face, Harmony knew that when Midnight woke up she wouldn't remember Harmony at all.

Midnight's memory would go back to before she saw Harmony walking out of the woods. After Harmony knew that it was done, she got up and left. The next morning, Midnight went downstairs to the kitchen, her parents looked up and asked where Harmony was. Midnight looked very confused and asked in return, "who is Harmony?". Now her parents looked confused, her mom quickly changed her expression from confused to pity and asked "hunny is this one of those things where you are asking because you don't want to talk about her?"

Midnight was still looking confused but replied, "no, I seriously have no idea who you are talking about". Her parents looked confused at each other and decided to bring Midnight to the one who helped her come out of her mother's stomach, Mary. When they got there Anna knocked on the door, when Mary opened the door and said, "Anna, Jax, Midnight, what a nice surprise". Anna quickly said, "you can call me Dial now, I am no longer ashamed of the name".

Jax spoke up as well, "well since you can call her Dial, you can call me Pepper". Mary just smiled, opened the door wider and stepped aside. The three of them walked in, while Midnight was talking to Jim, Dial and Jax were talking to Mary, Dial asked, "Mary, I think there might be something wrong with our daughter, could you please use a machine to look at her brain?" Mary looked confused but nodded and walked over to Midnight.

Mary spoke, "Midnight, would I be able to ask you to step inside my office please?" Midnight didn't ask any questions, she just nodded and sat in the patient's chair. Mary put a cap that had wires connected to it on Midnight's head, she flipped a switch and the scan started. Mary motioned for Dial to come over to her, Dial went over, and Mary started explaining what they were seeing. "There is a spot on her brain that I rarely see but I know what it is, this spot represents the erasing of part of her memory.

With that being said, someone either used magic or something else and erased her memory of something they didn't want her to remember. Do either of you know what and/or who did this?" After a moment had gone by, Dial spoke, "I know who, however, I don't know why, Harmony erased her mind, that explains why Midnight hasn't got the slightest clue as to who we are talking about." Pepper and Mary nodded their heads, Mary spoke again, "I'm going to tell you right now, if you want that part of Midnight's memory recovered the only way to do that is to have whatever happened, happen again.

That way it becomes a memory once again". "I know for a fact the neither one of us has any clue as to how to contact Harmony, so we just have to leave it alone and live on like she never existed" Dial said. Pepper and Dial took off the thing that was on Midnight's head, Midnight asked, "is there something wrong with me?" Dial shook her head no and they started walking back home after thanking Mary and Jim for taking the time to look Midnight over.

On their way home, there were animals all around them because it was now night time. Some of them growled some just walked but without even giving them a look. Just then a large pack of wolves not only out numbered them but circled them, Midnight went for the leader, who was the biggest one. The wolf had razor sharp claws and long pointed teeth, Dial shouted after Midnight to be careful. However, Midnight couldn't hear her because her and the wolf were already fighting.

Biting each other drawing blood with every scratch and bite, they fought for a little while, meanwhile Dial and Pepper were fighting all the rest. Both Midnight and the wolf were down to their last set of breaths, finally even though she was covered in hers and the wolf's blood, she took one final attacking lunge at the wolf and managed to claw his throat open with blood spitting and spilling everywhere. Midnight collapsed on the ground from exhaustion, her father carried a couple dead wolves home and her mother carried her home.

While Midnight was resting, Dial and Pepper sat in their bedroom and had a talk. Dial started with, "you know, it might sound horrible but if our daughter and myself end up dead you will find a way to live on without us, won't you?" "I don't know if I'll be able to, you and Midnight are the only ones I'm living for" Pepper replied. Dial spoke again, "then we need to find a way to make whatever time we have left, the best it can be.

I've never been to a waterpark or a beach, but I've heard a lot about them, we are going to all the ones that we can. We will use our eye powers to make them let us in without paying, hunny, we are gonna be living dangerously so get ready world because here we come". "Wait, wait, wait, before we go anywhere or do anything, don't you think we should talk to our daughter about this and see if we can do it as a family?" Pepper jumped in and asked.

The only thing Dial could reply with was, "yeah you're probably right", Dial went to Midnight's door and knocked, she cracked the door open to see if Midnight was awake yet. She was so Dial spoke, "hunny will you please get some clothes on and come downstairs, there is something that your father and I would like to talk to you about?" Midnight nodded and after her mom closed the door she got dressed and made her way down the stairs to find a glass of blood waiting for her, she sat down and took a couple sips.

Midnight looked at her parents and spoke, "so what's up you guys?" "hunny, your mother and I have decided that we would like to go places with you, as in waterparks, go see the ocean, have a long family vacation, what do you think of that?" Pepper replied. Dial jumped in and said, "don't worry about needing money, since we are not normal people we will use our eye powers to get people to let us in, what do you say Midnight? Do you want to come travel with us?"

Midnight slammed the rest of her glass of blood and then replied to their question, "well I don't have anything to live for here, why not". Dial piped up and said, "great, let's get packed and we will leave right away". Right after she said that there was a knock on the door, Midnight was the closest one, so she answered the door. "Hello, my name is James, my cellphone has died may I come in and borrow a phone, please?"

It was raining so he was drenched, Midnight quickly responded with, "you look familiar, have we met before?" What she didn't know was that James was the guy version of Harmony. When she stepped to the side to let James in, he walked by her and not only the look in his eyes, but his musk made her whole world slow down almost to a halt. James walked up to her parents and asked them what he asked her, but he slipped a note into Dial's hand when he shook it.

They gave him one of their cell phones, he walked into the kitchen and got busy with what he needed to do. Meanwhile Dial and Pepper were reading the note that James gave them, it read, "hello, I am the male version of Harmony, that's why your daughter feels like she knows me. I just hope that we are all in agreement that she will never ever find out, I will be facing you at this point, if you both agree just look up at me and nod".

That is exactly what they did when Dial shoved the piece of paper in her pocket, they both looked up and nodded. Midnight was still standing there with the door open, because she was trying to figure out where she knew that guy. It was still raining, her parents told her to shut the door before the floor gets all wet. James got done using the phone, handed it back and said, "their phones are off", what Midnight also didn't know is that when he handed it back he pushed a button and another note popped up, so Dial read that one too.

"I didn't actually try to call anyone, I just pretended to, so I could give y'all a moment or two to realize who I am". He looked up a Midnight who was just in awe at the sight of him, he cleared his throat and proceeded to ask another question. "Since it is raining and who I tried to call isn't answering, it's already dark out, may I stay the night here?" Without hesitation, Midnight immediately said, "yes". She slightly chuckled at what she had just done and said, "well what I meant was, if you would like to that would be fine.

I just need to tell you that we are a different kind of family". James spoke up once again but this time with a smile on his face, "Well thank you ma'am, and don't worry, I know that y'all are vampires, word travels fast". Midnight looked up at her parents, they smiled and nodded, then she looked back at James and she said while smiling and blushing "you can just call me Midnight. You can sleep in my room, I'll grab you our really comfy sleeping bag and a pillow".

James nodded and said, "thank you ma, I mean Midnight" he looked at Dial and asked, "may I have a glass of water please?" Dial not only nodded but got him a glass as well. As Midnight was getting the room set up, she wanted to keep staring at him but couldn't see him from her room. She quickly finished and headed downstairs to the kitchen where she sat next to him, a little closer than normal people sit by each other, but no one minded, not even James.

He finished his glass of water and spoke, "so Midnight, I think we should play a little game", she but in by asking, "ooh, what kind of game? Wrestling?" James chuckled and replied, "no

I'm sorry, I don't wrestle, especially not girls" Midnight giggled back and said, "oh me neither". James continued, "I was thinking that I could ask you a question, then you could ask me, and we just go back and forth like that until we run out of questions".

Midnight liked the idea so much that she said, "I'll go first, can we kiss?" James chuckled again but replied, "not yet, let's get to know each other first ok?" she nodded and said, "ok, your turn". "Ok, let's see, what to ask first, oh I know, how old are you?" "twenty-two", Midnight replied. "And how old are you?" Midnight asked, "I am also twenty-two" James replied. While they were playing the question game, Dial and Pepper were packing for the next day.

Midnight smiled at the fact that they were the same age, and James continued. "So, since I already know where you live, ha ha, what do you like to do for fun?" "Most of the time I like to just go outside and walk and think", Midnight replied. She continued, "Where do you live?" "I live in town, I'm so used to a lot of traffic that being out here in the country is a little strange", James replied. James but in before Midnight could say anything, "also I like to take walks but during the day and away from people".

They talked and talked and talked, they talked so long that it was almost three in the morning. They went to bed and when James woke up he was cuddling Midnight, he had a feeling that she would get on the floor to sleep next to him. She packed up her stuff and asked him to come with her and her parents on their long vacation. James stopped to think about it for a minute then spoke, "you know, I don't think anyone will be looking for me or miss me if I'm gone for a period of time.

However, you should know something........I'm human, and I don't care that you are a vampire". Midnight just smiled, she gave him a quick kiss and just waited. Luckily for her, he kissed her back and not only that, but they didn't just kiss, his tongue slipped into her mouth. She was a little shocked, but she let her tongue touch his, the kiss was getting heated, however, they didn't have sex yet, just a really good kiss. After the kiss, James looked at her and asked, "so are you ready to go?" Midnight smiled and said, "let's do it baby".

Midnight looked down at his hands, James noticed this and said, "I didn't have much where I was living anyway". "That's ok we can pick up some stuff for you on our traveling journey", Midnight replied.

Chapter 2

They were getting their stuff by the door when Midnight said, "wait, James can't run with us, he isn't a vampire. How is he going to keep up?", "well looks like we will have to buy a car after all", Dial replied. "Yeah, ok, and where are we gonna get that type of money?", Pepper asked in a slightly sarcastic tone. "We can ask the neighbor really nicely if we could borrow some money", Dial replied. "How will we pay them back?", Pepper asked a little agitated.

Dial said with a little bit of power in her voice, "we will work something out with them, don't worry about it". Off they went to talk to Mary and Jim, they went inside, explained what was going on and asked if there was a way that they could borrow money and work it off somehow or something. Mary and Jim looked and each other and nodded, then Jim spoke, scaring them a little at first, "I'll tell you what, you can borrow as much money as you need or want from us and in return".

He paused to let Mary finish telling them, "you have to send us post cards and knick-knacks from gifts shops and such until your debt is paid. How does that sound?", Mary asked with a smile. All Dial, Pepper, Midnight and James could do was smile.

Midnight went up and hugged Mary, then hugged Jim and said, "thank you, you have no idea what this means to my family". Mary just nodded at them and gave them an extra card to their account, Jim looked at her parents and said, "now you just call us if you have any problems.

You got that?" All of them nodded, they graciously took the card and headed out. The first thing they did when they got back home was make a small plan which was, for Dial and Pepper to go get a car that wasn't too flashy. Midnight and James were going to stay home and wait for them to get back. After that they were going to load up the car and go to the furthest waterpark in the U.S from them as they could, which was Florida.

They got piled in the car, once they got on the road they all smiled because it was the beginning of a very long adventure. The family would stop to hunt, and they would stop at restaurants so that James could eat as well. Since they didn't want to live too high of an adventure, they kept stopping at motels and resting. Obviously Dial and Pepper shared a bed, and for the first couple of motels, Midnight and James shared a bed but not blankets yet.

Although it felt like they've known each other for a very long time they were still kind of strangers. The very first place they stopped for a motel, they were able to find an antique store with not only post cards but also a gift for Mary and Jim from each one of them. Most of the motels they stopped at had a pool, so they were able to go swimming quite a bit. When Dial and Pepper or Midnight and James wanted some alone time, they'd have the other two go look for something for them.

Most of the time when Midnight and James were alone they

just talked, sometimes getting to know more about each other. Sometimes about a possible future, other times they would just sit, make-out and feed each other food. When Dial and Pepper were alone, sometimes it was sex, sometimes they would even spruce up the sex by trying new things and positions. Sometimes they would just talk about where they were going next.

A lot of the time they would just cuddle, eat junk food and watch tv. I know it sounds corny, and like a life no one would want to live, but all of them loved the life they were living, so far. All the fun they were having was about to majorly slow down if not stop, they were almost to Florida, when one of the motels they went to did background checks on the people who gave cards. When the clerk didn't like what they had seen, he went to talk to the manager or at least bring the manager to talk to the family.

The manager walked right up to the front desk and asked everyone for their ID's. Dial and Pepper looked at each other, nodded, and with a "not wanting to do it" sigh, Pepper got a little closer to the manager, and Dial to the clerk. They looked in their eyes and said with glowing red eyes, "you don't need to see any ID, you believe what you hear, you will give us a room for the length of time we are here. You will also not bother us again about this situation", once they were finished, their eyes went back to normal color and with a smile on the manager's face.

The gave them two room keys and said, "have a wonderful stay". The four of them went to their room, locked the door and Dial started freaking out. She started pacing the floor back and forth saying, "guys, I don't like what we just did, I don't like it at all. I'm really hoping that we won't have to be doing that a lot,

I have a feeling that it could eventually catch up to us". Pepper grabbed her shoulders looked her in the eyes and said, "as long as we are all together, will it really matter what happens to us?".

Dial looked shocked and mad at the same time said yelled, "of course it will! I do not plan on going to jail or prison just for trying to enjoy life with my family!" Pepper quickly replied with, "just calm down, I know that can be the worst thing a man can tell a woman but calm down. If you raise a stink about it especially around higher people like cops and such then things will get bad. I love you but please just keep calm until it happens, when it does, we will figure it out, we always will".

Pepper brought her in for a hug, she took a deep breath and said, "ok, you're right, let's continue our adventure". They once again continued giving each other "couple time", when they got to Florida, the first thing that Dial noticed was how the trees were just as someone had once described to her. They said that the trees are called palm trees. They described that the trunk of the tree was really tall, as tall as a light pole.

It doesn't have any branches, instead, it has really big leaves. These leaves are so big, if you pull one off you can use it to fan someone on a hot day. However, it's illegal to pull these leaves off the trees, and to get to the trees you have to use one of those machines that lift a person or people up. The machine goes really high, so if you are not afraid of heights, you'll be just fine. Now that they are in the state of Florida, they didn't want to stay in a motel.

Instead, they wanted to stay in a nice hotel, maybe with room service. Since Pepper was driving he decided to pull over and ask someone for directions to the nicest hotel in Florida. When they got to the hotel, there was someone to help take their bags, and someone to go park their car. None of them had heard of this so when the person came around to take the keys and park it, Pepper freaked out a little bit. He looked at the guy and said, "hey man, what are you doing, this is my car".

The man said, "if it's ok sir, I'd like to take your car and go park it. When you want to go somewhere just come outside, let me know and I'll go get it for you". Pepper thought that wasn't a bad idea, handed the man the keys and went around to the other side of the car. Their bags were on a cart, they walked up to the desk and asked for a simple room with room service. The clerk looked up at him and asked, "how many people?", Pepper was a little bit confused, so he asked just to clarify, "do you mean how many people are staying in the room?"

The clerk nodded, and Pepper replied with, "there are four of us". The clerk typed on her computer, she then asked what size of bed they would like. This time Dial looked confused and asked, "there are different sizes of beds?". The clerk looked up and slowly nodded, Midnight piped in and said, "could we please have two beds that will fit two people comfortably?" The clerk responded with, "sooo you want two queen beds in one room and room service.

Will that be all?" All four of them nodded, the clerk continued speaking, "and how long are you planning on staying with us?" James knew how to answer this one, so he replied with, "we aren't sure yet". The clerk quickly said, "it'll be eighty dollars a night, the room service will be added at the end of your stay". They all nodded again, Pepper pulled out the card that Mary and Jim gave them and went to the atm to get cash.

He took out one-hundred dollars, handed it to the clerk. She handed him twenty dollars back and once again he looked confused, he asked, "why are you giving me twenty dollars?" The clerk responded with, "I'm giving you your change sir, it costs eighty dollars and you gave me a one-hundred-dollar bill. That means that I give you twenty dollars back". Pepper looked at her, smiled and said, "thank you". Since there were four people (two couples), she only gave them two keys.

Before she let them go on their way she asked as politely as she could, "do you folks know how to use the keys?" All four of them looked at the keys they were given, looked back at the clerk and shook their heads no. The clerk then gently asked, "would it be ok if I show you how?" They all nodded with smiles, she took a key that would open the door behind her. Looked at the four of them and said, "ok now when you get to your door this is what you do.

Look for the arrow, make sure it is pointing down. Also, you want to make sure that it is facing you". She demonstrated what it meant to have it facing them and facing away from them, she then asked if they understood and once again they all nodded their heads yes. The clerk continued, "good, you have your keys, now you can go to your room. The number one the card should match the number on the door. When you get to your door, used one of the keys and do what I just showed you".

Once again they all looked at her and at the same time said, "thank you". They got to their room, Pepper pulled his key out of his pocket and did what the lady had shown them. It worked, they went inside and put their bags on the floor. Pepper and Dial called the first dibs on one of the beds, James and Midnight got the other bed. After they got their stuff inside the room and got settled they were going to go explore their surroundings.

Before they went to do that however, Pepper pulled James aside and said, "hey man, I think that now that we are in the state we were headed to, and we are in the room we are going to sleep in tonight we should give the girls a spa day. When we do that however, what are us guys gonna do?" James replied with, "that sounds like a great idea but that's also a good question". The first thing they could think of was look for an arcade, before they went to look for an arcade however, they went to the front desk.

The same lady was there, and she asked, "may I help you guys?" They politely asked, "is there a spa around here?" The clerk replied with, "yes gentle man in fact I have two tickets right here for an all day, spa. I'll make you a deal, I'll tell you what, I'll tell you about the spa and more about the hotel, on one condition. You stop bothering me, there will be someone here after seven o'clock". The two men nodded, she handed them the tickets and told them how to order room service.

She even told them about the buffet, the pool and the hot tub. When they were done talking to her, they met up with the girls, told them to close their eyes and hold out their hands. They did as they were asked, when the guys said, "open", they looked at the tickets and thought they were pretty but weren't sure what to do with them. Pepper explain what the clerk said, the girls nodded excitedly and raced off to the spa. The spa was at the other end of the hotel, they found someone else to ask them where the arcade was.

They wanted to make sure they got to the girls in time for the dinner buffet, meanwhile they headed straight to the arcade and started having the most fun they've had in their lives. They almost lost track of time but luckily Pepper decided to look at the clock, he thought to himself, "ok so the bar and buffet opens for dinner at seven o'clock. I know that Midnight and James will want to get there early, it's now six fifty".

He stopped what he was doing and told James it was time to go get the girls for the buffet, they raced to that end of the hotel. When they got their Dial, Pepper and Midnight had a little quiet conversation. They agreed, that even though they were vampires and all they wanted was blood and as raw of meat as they could have. They were going to eat what the buffet had, like normal people. Even though they were vampires, they wanted to appear normal as much as possible.

Hiding their real identities was the trickiest part of the trip, it was also the most fun. After they ate, they decided to go up to the room, put on their bathing suits and go swimming. Pepper and Dial wanted to actually swim, James and Midnight went in the hot tub. Dial sat down first, James sat across from her at first. They were giving each other sexy looks and Midnight said, "it's getting hot and steamy in here, you should move closer I can hear you over my parents swimming".

James smiled, moved closer slowly and said, "you're right, it is getting hot and steamy. Let's see if we can make it any hotter". They started kissing, Midnight put her hands on his face to keep him from pulling away. James put his hands on her waist and pulled her closer, there was only a sliver of space between them. They started making out more deeply, using their tongues and touching each other. Midnight was feeling up his warm wet arms and chest, James was putting his hands on her butt and occasionally squeezing.

While they were still in the water, James picked her up by the butt, she wrapped her legs around his waist. He sat down while holding her so that their bodies somewhat stayed in the hot water, they were still making out until his lips went down to her neck. He didn't care that her neck was wet, or that the fact that she was a vampire made her forever cold skinned. James started kissing her neck sweetly at first then he slightly started sucking on it, his hands were still on her butt.

She let out a quiet moan, she grabbed his face and they not only went back to making out, but they started making out harder. They were both getting horny and the hot tub started steaming up more, when heavy breathing started from both of them. James pulled away long enough to ask her, "do you want to go to the room and continue this?" Midnight gave him three more deep kisses then pulled away and nodded her head almost quickly.

They got up, got out of the hot tub, Midnight yelled to her mom saying that they were going to the room and to take their time. They grabbed their towels and were off to the room. When they got there, he shut and locked the door so not even her parents could get in. Midnight was facing away from him, she started undressing herself wanting to tease him. She was completely naked, she slowly grabbed a towel, wrapped it around herself, turned around and said, "if you want to see the front of me naked you'll have to come into the shower with me".

They went into the bathroom she stopped slowly dropped her towel, climbed into the shower and turned on the water. James got naked as well, and got in the back of the shower, she opened her eyes when she knew he was in there and smiled. He got closer to her, he slightly squeezed her breasts, she grabbed his waist and pulled him close this time. They started making out again, he went to her neck again, this time he was sucking a little harder.

She let out a louder moan but neither one of them cared, he kept sucking on her neck, wanting to make sure he gave her a good-sized pleasure bruise. She kept moaning and getting louder, James shut off the shower water. Opened the curtain, they grabbed hands when they were walking to the bed. They stopped at the end of the bed, they were naked, wet and making out. James gently sat her on the bed, had her lay down and scoot up towards the pillow.

He slowly started crawling towards her, she got off the bed, went to the end of the bed and told him to lay down where she was. Midnight crawled up this time, she started at his belly button, slowly kissing up his chest. This was making him rock hard, when he couldn't take it anymore, he grabbed her face and brought her in for a lot more kissing. She sat in the perfect spot on him and started moving her hips back and forth.

They were making out, breathing heavily, and she was moving her hips in just the right way. When he once again couldn't take it anymore, he flipped them over, slid his penis inside her and started thrusting. Slowly at first, then he started going faster, she was loving the love she was getting, she didn't want it to stop. They were making out while having amazing sex, to tease her, he stopped and just slightly started sucking on her neck again.

This time she couldn't take it anymore, she flipped them over and started riding him. They were both breathing heavy and moaning a little, she was riding as fast as she could. James held her hips in place when he came, then just started smiling at her, she was smiling back. Midnight bent down to give him a couple more kisses, then got off the bed so they could wipe up and get dressed. After they got dressed James started kissing her again, after a couple kisses, she pulled away and said, "if we kiss like we were kissing, we are gonna end up doing that again".

James smiled and whispered in her ear, "is that a bad thing?" This made her whole-body tingle and with trying to catch her breath she said, "not necessarily". They smiled, kissed again, hugged, and went down to see her parents.

Chapter 3

They sat by the pool while her parents were still swimming. It was starting to get late so Midnight decided to say, "hey mom, dad, it's almost time for the pool to be closed for the night. We should probably go up to the room for the night, we can come back tomorrow". Her parents looked at her and her mom said in return, "you guys go ahead, we will be there in a bit". Midnight was thinking that maybe they wanted to make out in the pool a little bit before going to bed, so her and James went to the room.

Since they had already had sex, they decided to not only share the bed but also the blanket that was on it. She didn't want to sleep naked because they were in a hotel room, so she slept in her underwear and a tank top. Midnight crawled into bed under the covers and smiled when James crawled in from the other side. They were under the covers, getting close to each other and in their underwear. She put her hand on his cheek, he put his hand on her hip.

Midnight decided to ask him, "so we haven't made us, official". She was still smiling, waiting for a response. James smiled and responded, "Midnight, I would absolutely love it, if you would be mine, my girlfriend, my everything". Midnight was smiling even bigger now, this is how she responded, "this will give you my answer". She pulled him as close to her as she could and gave him the most passionate kiss she could.

James was happy about her answer, so he kissed her right back. They were still kissing when her parents came into the room, her mom said, "don't worry, we are coming in with our shut, so you don't have to worry about us seeing anything". Midnight just giggled and said in reply, "it's ok guys we are under the covers and not even completely naked". They opened their eyes and was deciding which one was going to go first, Dial said, "if we take one together, we risk shower sex".

Pepper replied in return, "and with that being said, ladies first". This made Dial smile and blush, she brought her bathroom stuff into the bathroom along with her pajamas which came off when she got into bed. Dial showered, and then Pepper showered, even though it kind of felt awkward for all of them, Dial and Pepper were making out in bed and so were Midnight and James. When Midnight had had enough, she rolled over and scooted back so the back of her was touching James.

They cuddled, and Midnight fell asleep with his arms wrapped around her. Dial and Pepper did the same thing and they both felt something they hadn't felt in a very long time. What was it you ask? It was the romance that Dial thought had died a long time ago, back when they just had Midnight. All of a sudden, Pepper had the most bizarre and crazy thought. He randomly spoke up when they were all just sitting around the room, "y'all know what we should do?

We should go on a massive killing spree; however, we should

obviously start in a small town, so we can run to a bigger town when we are done". The rest of them looked at each other, the girls were looking at each other and saying, "I don't think we should do that. We should just enjoy life". Meanwhile James was looking at Pepper with a smile and said, "I think we absolutely should do that. We could become the crazy family that killed an entire nation".

Pepper responded to James with, "now that is what I call, thinking to the future". Dial suddenly stood up with her hands up saying, "whoa, whoa, whoa, we aren't actually thinking about doing this are we? This is just a really sick joke that you two guys are talking about, right?" Pepper and James just looked at each other, Pepper then turned to Dial and responded with, "Hun, we are being completely serious right now". Dial's jokingly smile faded and she spoke again, "Pepper, just because we are vampires doesn't mean we should go around killing people.

We just need to keep feeding off of human food and animals like we have been". Pepper responded with, "Dial, because we are vampires is the reason we should start a killing spree". Dial got slightly mad and said, "Pepper, you are forgetting one small detail......James isn't a vampire. He is completely human who is in love with our daughter who IS a vampire". Pepper spoke, "but James is even agreeing to go along side vampires and kill a bunch of people".

Dial turned to James and asked, "are you going to say anything about this?" James looked and Dial and responded with, "I've just been waiting for my turn to speak. I love running with vampires, besides, I don't have any family or anything to go back to. I don't care what I have to do to stay running with vampires, I'll kill as many people as I have to". Pepper raised his hands to calm down James and said, "ok calm James, you don't have to prove yourself to stay with us".

He turned back to Dial and asked, "are you satisfied now?" Dial thought for a moment then smiled a smartass smile and asked, "ok, here is another problem for you then, who is going to carry him when we have to run from cops? And don't tell me that he can ride in the back of the car because you and I both know we won't be getting away in a car". Without hesitation Midnight stood up and before anyone could say anything she said, "I'll do it, I'll carry him.

Mom I'm sorry to say this but you were the only one who was against the idea of a massive slaughter". Midnight looked at James, held his hands and said, "the reason I want to, is because I have a very good feeling that it'll strengthen our relationship". Midnight smiled, then James smiled, once Pepper could see the happy faces then he smiled. Dial looked at all of them and said rather quickly, "so let me get this straight, I am the only one who doesn't like the thought of murdering a bunch of innocent people?"

The three of them looked at each other, then at her and nodded. Dial did a big sigh and just stood there quietly, Midnight knew that her mother was contemplating the decision of going along with it or not. So, Midnight walked up to her mother, gave her the puppy dog face and started making a puppy begging noise. Her mother just looked at her and thought, "really, are you seriously begging me to go along with a mass murder right now?"

Dial did a big sigh, looked around at everyone at finally said, "ok, ok, we can kill". The three of them at once said, "yes", as if they achieved something. Dial quickly spoke again, "but how are we even going to start this mass murder?" They all looked puzzled, then the funniest thing happened, they watched a couple of horror movies to learn what to do. After watching their last horror film, Pepper stood up and said, "well, we will go to the dollar store and pick up some chloroform, rags, and gardening tools.

The tools will be for a slow torture, most of the movies we have watched has had slow torture in them". The other three dropped their jaws and looked at him and shock, he then said, "hey it was the movies that gave me the ideas". Midnight and James started laughing and then Midnight said, "dad, that is awesome". Pepper then put his hands on his hips, looked up at a diagonal and said, "it's settled, we will start tomorrow.

As soon as the store opens, we will go get our supplies and head to the closest small town. A town that barely even has a police station, after we have killed everyone in the town, we will go to the next town but a size up. We will do this until we hear from the cops "hey, stop right there!" Then Midnight will pick up James and we will run". Once he stopped talking, James and Midnight stood up and applauded him. After the applause was done, her parents kissed her on the forehead and went to bed.

Pepper made sure to wake up early the next morning, so he could prepare to never be the same vampire again. It was roughly ten minutes to when the store would be opening, he got James awake and ready to go. They headed to the store and got all the supplies they needed, they were relieved when the cashier didn't ask them any questions about the items. When they got back to the hotel, the girls were already awake so naturally the guys gave their girl kisses.

The girls got ready to go, they all went over the plan again and left the hotel. Pepper decided to stop and ask someone if they knew where the closest small town was. The nice stranger nodded their head, pointed and said, "about 20 miles that way. Y'all might be able to see one of them desert hay balls rolling across the street". Pepper smiled and said, "thank you". The stranger smiled, nodded, and kept walking. After he got the window rolled back up he said to the whole car, "that sounds like our perfect start".

Everyone smiled except for Dial she was still not one hundred percent on board with the whole idea. As they were getting further out, James could barely make out a farm that was out in the middle of no-where. He pointed it out and Pepper drove to it. When they got there, there were two vehicles there, Pepper and James got out of the car so that the men could do the hard stuff first. Which was knocking the folks out and dragging their bodies to the closest bedroom with a head-board.

Pepper knocked on the door and a nice woman answered, she said, "yes, may I help you?". Pepper, as politely as he could, asked, "excuse me ma'am, is your husband home with you?". She then worriedly asked if he had done something wrong, Pepper slightly giggled and responded with, "no ma'am. We would just like to speak to you both at the same time if y'all don't mind". The woman was a tad bit confused but called her husband to the door, which luckily for the guys he was very thin and looked like he was light.

Each of the guys had the chloroform filled rags in their back pockets ready to go, when the man got to the door he put his hands on his hips, looked at the men and asked, "is there something we can help you guys with?". James looked at Pepper, looked back at the couple and with a smile on his face said, "well actually yes", the guys then wiped out the rags and stuffed them in the couples faces. They obviously struggled for a good little bit, but luckily there was enough chemical on the rags to knock them both out.

The guys gently laid them on the floor, they didn't want to be rude and let them just drop. Once they got the couple to the bed and tied up, they went to the front door and signaled for the ladies to come in. The girls went into the house with the bag full of tools and headed for the bathroom, so they could sterilize them. After all the tools were sterilized, they went to the bedroom, since the chemical took about an hour to wear off, they had a sandwich and waited.

The couple started waking up, James was finishing his third sandwich by this time. The girls grabbed their tools and waited for them to start freaking out, the man woke up first but didn't scream. The girls looked at each other confused and asked why he wasn't screaming or calling out for help. The man very calmly responded with, "well miss, we are in the middle of no-where, haven't seen a cop out here in ten, maybe fifteen years.

I don't figure there'll be one here now, so might as well save my energy. Also, I know that if I end up dead, I will be going to visit the Lord almighty". Dial looked shocked and didn't know what to say, Midnight on the other hand stood up, and as fierce as she could, pointed the sharp object at him and said, "damn right you'll end up dead. Both you and your wife are gonna die, today".

James and Pepper tried not to laugh at her trying to be all tough with a gardening tool in her hand. She knew this and so to prove that she was tough, she cut the man on his face then on his chest. The man screamed, the guys had shocked expressions and one of them said, "I didn't think she would or could actually do it". Pepper spoke again right after that and said, "well, I'm proud of you baby girl". Midnight smiled and said, "thank you".

When the man screamed, it woke his wife up, she didn't have the same mentality, so she started screaming as soon as she realized what was going on. This made James and Pepper smile, her husband out voiced her and yelled, "dog gonnit Miriam, we're in the middle of nowhere. The only way a cop is gonna know what is happening is if we go to town and tell'em. I hate to break it to you, but I don't think we are going anywhere, anytime soon".

She stopped screaming and yelling and just started crying, she wasn't crying at the fact that they were tied up and about to die however, she was crying at the fact that her husband just yelled at her even though he didn't cuss at her. He apologized, and she was able to stop crying and say, "thank you, after the last five years of marriage, thank you Bufford, for finally apologizing to me". He rolled his eyes and said in an annoyed tone, "your welcome Miriam".

Dial spoke up and said, "well now that we know their names, should we introduce ourselves. Considering the fact that we are the last faces they will ever see?" The four of them looked at each other, James stepped forward, so the couple could see them and said, "My name is James and I'm a human". After James stepped back, Pepper stepped forward and said, "My name is Pepper and

I'm a vampire". Dial and Midnight remained seated, Midnight went first and said, "I'm Midnight and I am also a vampire".

Then it was Dial's turn to speak, "well folks, my name is Dial and I am a vampire as well. I am married to Pepper and James and my daughter are together". The couple said, "nice to meet you", Miriam continued with saying, "I wish we were meeting on better terms, but nice to meet y'all". They all just sat there quietly for a moment then Midnight stood up again and asked, "well should we get this thing going or what?".

No one wanted to see the couple naked, so she just started cutting the woman's face, Bufford finally said, "please don't hurt her, you can hurt me all you want. For the love of the almighty, please leave her alone". Miriam got a tear in her eye both because the cutting hurt and because of what he husband had just said, but Midnight continued to cut, just in different places. Miriam was able to turn her head to Bufford and Bufford to Miriam. They looked at each other for a moment then Bufford said, "well Miriam, it's been a mighty fine pleasure, living life with the most beautiful woman I know and love. I'll see you on the other side".

Chapter 4

With a tear in her eye, Miriam just looked at Bufford and smiled. Dial, with a tear in her eye as well, stood up and said, "ok now you see guys this is exactly the reason we should kill anyone. Because there are good people out there like Miriam and Bufford". She paused for a moment, the other three looked at each other, at the same time said, "nah", and Midnight went up and stabbed Bufford in the leg. Dial covered her mouth in shock, the guys were smiling and hi-fiving each other, and Bufford was trying to breathe through the pain.

He didn't want to scream because he knew that, that would freak Miriam out even more. When blood started spurting everywhere, Miriam started screaming. She was a tiny bit squeamish at the sight of blood, and that is not being sarcastic. It was a hand shovel that Midnight had stabbed him with, so it looked like something with really smooth teeth had bit him with only it's top teeth. To make it look like a full-teeth bite she decided to turn the tool around, go up his leg about a half inch and stabbed.

Bufford still didn't scream, instead he just kept trying to breath while his wife was the one freaking out. Miriam finally asked him, "how are you not screaming in pain, doesn't it hurt?". He snickered for a moment then replied, "Miriam, it hurts like you would not believe. I'm just trying to stay as calm as I can so that you don't start freaking out more than you already are". Miriam didn't know what to say so she just looked at the ceiling and started crying, when she took a breath she was still staring at the ceiling but asked, "why are you crazy people doing this?".

Since it was Pepper's idea, he decided to say, "because we want to mix up our lives a little bit". Miriam spoke again, "but you are vampires and a human, isn't it mixed up enough? You could travel, see the world, why do you have to kill us?" Pepper replied with, "we aren't just killing you folks, we are planning on killing lots and lots of people. We've already traveled literally across the nation, so we figured", Dial cleared her throat and looked at him, he continued, "well I figured that we could mix it up more.

So now we are killing people until we have to run". Miriam didn't like that answer so she started crying again. Midnight was looking at the bloody shovel and smiling, she looked at how Bufford's leg had been stabbed but not Miriam's. So, she decided to stab Miriam's leg in the exact same spot but on the opposite leg. Miriam started scream crying now, from the pain. Once again, Bufford said but louder this time, "please for the love of God, don't hurt her, just me!"

Midnight walked over to him and said, "now that wouldn't be fair if we just hurt one and not the other, now would it?" Bufford gave her an evil look, she slapped him for that. Midnight then turned around and asked, "does anyone else want a turn for torture?" They all shook their heads no, she turned back to the couple. looked Bufford in the eyes again and said, "well then in that case, since you want me to spare her life here is what I will do".

She didn't tell him, she just walked around the bed to Miriam's side, tickled Miriam's body with the shovel and paused. She looked at Bufford who was watching her every move, started begging her not to do anything. She looked back at Miriam and said, "don't worry, your husband will be joining you soon enough". She then suddenly stabbed the shovel into Miriam's wind pipe and left it there, she left it there because she knew that if she ripped it out, Miriam would quickly bleed to death.

She waited for a moment then asked Bufford, "would you like me to now end your wife's suffering?" Bufford started crying and frantically shook his head in agreement, she looked back at Miriam and said, "goodbye sweet lady", and ripped the shovel out. Blood started spurting out everywhere, while it was spurting up, it was also running down the rest of her neck. Ran down shoulders and onto the bed under her. Bufford squeezed his eyes shut and kept them shut the moment Midnight went to touch the shovel, he couldn't bear to watch his wife die.

While he was squeezing his eyes shut, tears came out and ran down his face. It looked like some was trickling a small stream of water down the side of his face. He was starting not to be able to breath because he was crying so hard, so Midnight blew on his face to remind him to breathe. He took a deep breath but continued to cry, at this point he still didn't see a reason to scream for help. Bufford knew that this was his end, the only person or people who could save him now were the people doing the torturing.

When he was able to get a couple words out, he pleaded, "please, just finish me so I can go be with my wife". Midnight went over to her dad and asked him to chloroform him so that they could take him to a darker room, Pepper agreed and did so. When Bufford woke up, his face was all bloody and bruised from a face beating while he was unconscious, and he was just in boxers. His hands were strapped to the chair he was now sitting in, and his ankles were strapped as well.

Bufford was bald, so Midnight couldn't torture by pulling hair, instead she did some of the worst things she could to him. With tools like fence cutters, big, long, bulky scissors, and other tools. He screamed and screamed in pain, he was ok with screaming now because he no longer needed to be strong for his wife. When he was just about dead, he had a couple of breathes left so Midnight decided to just let him sit, bleed and die.

Bufford's last words were, "I'm coming my dearest Miriam". That brought a tear to Dial's eyes. With one final exhale he was gone. Once all the torturing was done, and the man was dead, the four of them decided that they should at least be respectful and burry the bodies close together. They buried the bodies, said a couple words and left. When they left they almost felt awkward about torturing and killing an innocent couple then giving them a somewhat nice funeral.

The only one who decided to speak up was Dial and she said, "I told y'all we should not be doing this". Pepper quickly piped in and said, "the only reason we are feeling like this is because we are first time murderers. Once we get a couple more in, we should feel completely crazily normal". The car once again fell silent, no one said anything until they got to the nearest small town. They went to the police station, Pepper said, "ok, it's my turn now, I'm going in".

He got out of the car and went in, he saw that there was a receptionist, a chief deputy sheriff, and an officer. The three of them were standing around the receptionists desk, chatting up a storm. Pepper cleared his throat but not in a rude way, and he wanted to be taken seriously so he was going to tell them that his name was Jax, instead of Pepper. He spoke when he had the sheriff's attention, "excuse me, could you possibly come outside and help me with a situation?"

None of them thought anything of it, so the sheriff agreed. The officer went to go take a nap, and the receptionist decided to play on her phone. No one knew that Pepper had a big knife in the back of his jeans, when they got outside, and the sheriff's back was facing Pepper. Pepper grabbed the knife from behind him, and with the very hard end of the handle, hit the sheriff in the back of the head as hard as he could and knocked him out.

Since they had a car they weren't quite sure how they were going to transport the sheriff, since the backseat was already in use. Pepper flicked his thumb up to Dial as a signal for her to pop the trunk, she did, and she had James go help him get the sheriff inside. Once that was done Pepper went back inside to tell the receptionist, "the sheriff went for a walk. However, he told me to come inside and get the officer to come help with the rest of the problem. Would that be ok?"

She nodded her head and went to go get him, they both came back and the officer started heading outside with Pepper to the car. Pepper did the same thing the officer as he did with the sheriff, then went inside for the last time to talk to the receptionist. "Excuse me miss, but when the sheriff came back, both him and the officer said that one of the small problems that I am having could only be handled by you. They suggested I come get you, so we could be on our way".

She nodded, put her phone down and followed him outside. Pepper chloroformed her, just to be a less aggressive gentleman. Once they had the three bodies in the trunk, Pepper drove back to the farm that they had started the killings at. The sheriff was the lucky one to be strapped to the chair in the spotlight, the receptionist and the officer were tied to the bed. The receptionist was a light sleeper anyway, so she was the first one to wake up.

Of course, she started freaking out because the last thing she remembered was going outside to help a man with a problem he was having. She started asking questions like, "who are you people? What's going on? Where am I?" She only saw the girls, because the guys were in the other room with the sheriff. Dial spoke up and said, "relax Hun, my husband is the one you were talking to before he knocked you out".

She looked confused and frightened, she turned her head and noticed that the officer was still asleep or unconscious she wasn't sure. She rolled her eyes and said, "well he will probably be out for quite a few hours. What did you guys do with the sheriff, is he dead?" Midnight spoke up this time and said, "no, no, no, no one is dead………yet". Once again the poor woman looked at the girls in horror, but this time she started crying.

The receptionist started begging them to either let her go or just finish her off. Dial and Midnight looked at each other, then looked back at the woman and Midnight said, "since you are the only woman that has begged, and we are only gonna do the requests of the women, we will just kill you. No torture". The woman started crying a little harder and choked out the question, "why do I have to die?" Dial replied, "because unfortunately you have been caught in our mass slaughter, we are planning on killing a lot of people in a lot of states".

Midnight looked at her mother with happy shock that she has finally said something about what they are doing. Something besides, "we shouldn't do this". The woman looked shocked and continued to cry, Midnight finally had enough of her crying. She took her butcher knife, walked over to the crying woman and asked for her name. The woman was able to choke out, "Lauren". Midnight looked her in the eyes and said, "it's been nice to meet you Lauren".

She then slit Lauren's throat, Dial and Midnight watched her bleed out from her neck. While she was bleeding out, Midnight noticed that the officer's nostrils were twitching, as if he was smelling something. He opened his eyes and started freaking out because he was tied up. He was looking around, looked to the side of him and saw that Lauren had just finished bleeding out. He started screaming almost as loud as he could, Midnight was able to yell above him and yell, "shut up!"

It took a few minutes, but she was finally able to get him

quiet. He started asking the same questions everyone does when they wake up tied up. Midnight looked at her mom and asked, "would you like to do this whole round, do you just want to fill him in, or do you just want to sit and watch?" Dial thought for a moment then responded, "I'll fill him in, I'll go get a sandwich and then I'll sit here and watch you have fun". They nodded at the same time, Dial got up, walked over to him and filled him in.

She then went to the kitchen to make a sandwich, during her sandwich making she could hear somewhat girly screeches. When Dial got back to the room, Midnight had made a few cuts to the officer's face. As usual, the victim was begging to be released. Saying, "I'll do anything you want, give you anything you want". Midnight said, "the only thing we want is to torture and kill people, like we explained before".

Once again he started begging to be released, almost tearing up from fear. Dial had enough so she punched him as hard as she could and stole the sharp pocket knife from Midnight's pocket. She started slitting the officer's throat, but Midnight pulled her hand away and said, "we aren't doing that yet". Dial looked aggravated but walked back to the chair after handing Midnight back the knife. She sat down and said, "fine, get on with it then, this one is annoying". Midnight not only smiled, but she also chuckled a little bit.

She turned back to the officer, leaned in a little closer and asked, "so what is your name, officer?" He looked confused but answered, "Daniel, my name is officer Daniel". Midnight looked at her mom and nodded, as if to tell her mom to go write the name down. That is exactly what she went into the kitchen to do.

She had just gotten done writing the name down, when she was startled by a man's scream coming from another room.

Dial knew that it was the sheriff, but she was curious, so she went to see what they had done to him. She peeked around the door and was a little shocked to see that they had cut off his penis. Dial went back to the room, told Midnight, and with the smile on Midnight's face, she knew she was going to do the same. Midnight didn't care how they did it, she just knew how she was going to. She grabbed a pair of scissors that could grab a pole and placed it around the penis, she then as slowly as she could, cut at the base.

Just a hair above the sack, when it started hurting him, she smiled and kept going. Midnight had finally snipped it off then gently laid it next to him and watched him bleed out. When he was done bleeding out, the house was silent because there were no more victims screaming. The victims stopped screaming because they were dead. Dial started cleaning up her area, and Pepper and James were cleaning up theirs. They all agreed on one thing, after every torture was done, they would give all the victims a proper burial.

They moved the dead bodies outside, so they could clean up their areas. Get the bed clean, the tools, the ropes and anything else they used. Then after that was done they decided burry the two males completely naked, they dressed the woman in clean clothes. They buried them next to the other two that they had killed, one grave at a time, they all said a few words. They went to the next grave, said a few words, and the next. Once all the words had been spoken, they packed up their things and went to the next town.

It was going to be awkward in the vehicle for a little bit, after each killing. Only because they all knew that killing was wrong, but it was now a way of life. After they knocked out the victims, they looted the bodies and got them in place and tied up. They slowly became pocket rich, they knew however that even if they got five dollars here and five dollars there, it would add up. They didn't necessarily care about the money, it was more just the sick thrill of the tortures.

Chapter 5

One innocent town after another, they knocked out, looted, tortured, killed and buried. All but Dial never once stopped and thought that they could stop and have material things. Such as a nice house, cell phones, maybe even human jobs. Especially Pepper and Midnight were now hooked on the new life style, James was still just going along with it. The car was quiet as they were driving to their fifth town, Pepper piped up and said, "you know, I just had a thought.

Once we are all filled up on what we are doing, we should turn ourselves in. Since we write all the names of our victims down, and we know where we burry them. It'll be easier for the law enforcement to put us away". He went silent waiting for a response, Dial was the first one to respond. She said, "Hun, that is the first sensible thing you have said since we started this". That made Pepper smile, James and Midnight agreed with what Pepper and Dial had said.

They came to their fifth town, Midnight spotted a bar, so she suggested to go there. When they got parked and started going inside there was a woman right outside the door crying. Her friend was trying to calm her down and ask her what happened, the woman managed to choke out, "my parents have been murdered and buried in their own backyard". Dial was curious, so she went over and decided to speak to the woman, "excuse me ma'am, I'm so sorry to disturb your mourning but may I ask a couple questions?"

The weeping woman nodded her head, so Dial started her questioning, "what was your parents name's?" The woman choked out, "Miriam and Bufford". Dial's first thought was, "oh crap", she then said, "I am so sorry for your loss, excuse me". She went back inside and let the woman mourn her parents, she frantically tapped on pepper's shoulder. He turned around and asked her what the problem was, she said, "the woman outside that's weeping, she just lost he parents".

He looked at her slightly confused and asked, "ok, that's sad but nothing we can do about it". She gave him a look and said, "we are the ones that murdered her parents, in fact they were our first victim". Pepper went closer to her ear and whispered, "Hun, we need to act calm and not look like we've been killing. I don't know about you but I'm not ready to go to prison yet, just stay calm, I'll let you know when it's a good time to be freaking out".

Dial nodded, went up to the bar and asked, "could I get four shots of moonshine, or something as strong please?" The bartender nodded his head, got her the four shots and said, "when you drink these, you might want to be sitting". Dial nodded said, "thank you", and turned around with the shots in her hands. The three of them looked at her confused, so when they didn't take them right away she said, "these are shots of moonshine or something as strong.

I think we each need to sit down and take one, that way we won't be suspicious". They all nodded, sat down, and clinked their shots together. One at a time they slammed down the shot and put the glass back on the table. Dial smiled and then said, "alright, now let's have some fun". The rest of them smiled and that is exactly what they did that night. Midnight woke up the next morning handcuffed to a bed half naked, James was on the floor stomach side down.

He was naked except for socks, and he had a bottle upside down looking like his butthole was drinking. He was still breathing so Midnight didn't need to be worried about that part, she looked at her hands and only one of them were handcuffed. All of a sudden there was a knock at the door and a voice that called out, "room service!" Midnight frantically said, "please, please come in!" So, the maid did and was shocked by the man on the floor.

She was going to run out of the room, but Midnight said, "no, no, wait, please don't go". The maid stopped and looked at her hand being handcuffed, and asked, "would you like some help?" Again, Midnight frantically nodded her head. The maid helped her, grabbed dirty stuff from the room minus clothing, and left. Midnight was able to wake James up and at least get a blanket around him since they had no idea where his clothes were.

They sat for a moment and let their headaches die down a little bit then Midnight said, "we need to figure out where mom and dad are. We also need to figure out what happened last night, I just remember taking the shot of moonshine". James nodded, Midnight got dressed, her and James walked slowly down the stairs in the hall. They got to the bottom and discovered that they were in the bar, the bartender that was there last night was there again.

Midnight walked up to the bar and asked, "excuse me, I know that you are the bartender from last night. You got my mother four moonshine drinks, do you remember?" The bartender nodded his head and spoke, "yeah I remember, your mom was hot. If your going to ask me if I know where she is, the answer is no. However, she left this note, drunk off her ass of course, and then she and the man she was with left. I saw them get into a cab".

Midnight thanked her, took the note, and went and sat by James. The note she read said, "best motel in the town". She nudged James, and they left. They got into a cab and Midnight asked, "could you please take us to the best motel in town?" The cab driver asked in return, "the woman from last night, are you her daughter?" Midnight frantically nodded her head, the cab driver continued, "I thought you were familiar, you have her face and her sober voice".

The cab driver dropped them off, they went inside, and the clerk motioned for them to go to her. They got there, and she asked, "are you the daughter?" Midnight nodded her head, the clerk handed her the second room key and said, "she wouldn't quit talking about how much she loves her family and named them all. Especially you". Midnight smiled, thanked the clerk and her and James headed towards the room number that was on the key.

They got there but knocked before entering, even though she had a feeling they weren't going to like what they saw when they entered anyway. They entered, luckily they were both in there, but so was another person. This person had a mask on, Midnight and James walked and looked around the room. She noticed that there was a note on the bedside table that read, "I'll get you after I get your daughter", it was signed, "the person in the mask".

She was able to wake her mother up who was passed out naked on the bed face down, her left arm and left leg were hanging off the side of the bed. Her face was facing the same direction, towards the window. Once she was awake, she asked what happened. Midnight asked what she remembered, she responded, "all I remember was taking a shot of moonshine". The three of them started giggling, the giggle woke Pepper up, this time he was the one freaking out.

He was asking why he was tied to a chair in only his boxers. Midnight held back another giggle and said, "probably because the person who took advantage of all of us left you like that. Then decided to pass out staring at you two". Midnight helped her mother up, so she could help her husband out of the chair, he was then able to put some pants on, so he wasn't just in his boxers. They gathered as much stuff that was theirs as they could and left, although the housekeepers probably wouldn't have cared if they took more.

Once they were all outside, Pepper stopped and asked, "well now what do we want to do?, we could either continue killing or we could find something else to do". As they started walking down the street Midnight had a sudden urge to puke, she ran into the alley next to them and puked behind the dumpster. James was right there to make sure she was ok and to make sure there wasn't any puke in her hair. Once she was done puking she took a deep breath and let it out slowly, she and James walked back to Pepper and Dial.

Midnight looked at all of them and said, "since I'm a vampire I think we should go see Mary to figure out why I just puked". The rest of them looked at each other and nodded, they got in their vehicle and drove back to the other side of the country. Once they pulled up to Mary and Jim's Dial knocked on the door, behind her was Midnight that had a bag full of souvenirs. She had still been throwing up almost the whole way there, she was having a very hard time keeping anything down.

Mary opened the door with a slight smile not expecting to see Dial and her family. It took Mary a moment to realize who was at the door, when she did, her face went from a slight smile to completely shocked and excited. Mary opened the door wide and let them all in, once all were inside Mary as politely and friendly as she could asked, "what can I do for y'all?" Midnight spoke up and said, "I've been puking all day for some weird reason".

Mary looked at her and asked, "would it be ok with you if I brought you into the ultrasound room?" Midnight nodded, grabbed James's hand and followed Mary to the room. Dial and Pepper stayed behind to chat with Jim, Mary kept the computer screen facing her only. Midnight and James waited patiently to find out why Midnight started puking. Mary then said, "James, you may want to come over here". So, James walked over to Mary to see what was on the screen.

When he looked, he grew a very shocked expression on his face. Him and Mary exchanged looks and then James looked at Midnight and said, "Babe, I'm not sure how to tell you this but, you're pregnant". Midnight blinked a couple times and said, "I'm sorry, what did you say James?" "you are pregnant", James said again. "How can that be?, we haven't had made love that much. Plus, there is only one in a million chance that I could've gotten pregnant seeing that I'm a vampire and you're a human".

Once the ultrasound goo was all cleaned off of Midnight's belly, she and James walked out to Dial and Pepper. Dial stood up from where she was sitting and anxiously looked at Midnight, she didn't say anything because Midnight was about to say something. Midnight looked up at her mom and said, "mom, dad.......... you're gonna be grandparents". Dial was so shocked she couldn't speak but Pepper quickly said, "I'm sorry I don't think we heard you correctly, will you please repeat what you just said?"

Midnight walked closer to them and said, "I, your daughter, am pregnant. That means, you're gonna be grandparents and James and I are gonna be parents". After taking a moment to wrap her head around what her daughter had just told her, Dial grew a big smile. She gave Midnight a big hug, started crying and said, "hunny, that's amazing, I didn't think I was ever going to get the chance to be a grandma". After looking over the ultrasound thoroughly, Mary came out, looked at Midnight and said, "you may want to sit down".

Midnight looked confused but sat down, Mary pulled a chair closer to Midnight, and sat down with some pictures in her hand. Mary then spoke and said, "the fetus looks good and healthy so far, you will still be able to give birth. However, I'm not sure how long your child will live after birth". Every one took a moment to wrap their heads around what was just said, then Midnight spoke, "mom, dad, you two should continue the vacation.

We can send postcards back and forth, James and I will stay here where I can grow our child and have the safest delivery possible". Dial opened her mouth to say something but Midnight put her hand up like a stop sign to silence her. That didn't work so Midnight began talking louder than her mother after hearing her mother start saying, "no, we are staying here with you", she was able to cut her mother off. "Mom, James and I will be ok here, we have the best doctor I know.

Plus, when you send me your postcards, just tell me what the next town you will be going to is, that way I can mail you a letter letting you know that your grandchild has arrived". Dial went to say something else but Pepper put his hand on her shoulder as a way to silence her, him putting his hand on her shoulder also said, "just let it go hunny. Our daughter has already made up her mind". Dial stayed quiet, and put her head down in sadness knowing that she was going to be leaving her only child behind.

Meanwhile she and her husband were going to be out and about having fun all around the country, she was not happy, obviously. Dial hugged her daughter tightly, then walked out the door with tears rolling down her cheeks. Pepper hugged her as well but not as tightly, and asked, "would you like us to send you pictures of the dead bodies?" Midnight nodded her head, hugged her dad back and watched him walk out the door.

Even though she wanted to go with him she knew that it would be better for her and the fetus inside her to stay where they were. The four of them walked home, Dial and Pepper packed a few things to carry because they would no longer be needing the car. Midnight and James packed two big duffel bags because they were going to be staying with Mary and Jim until the baby came. Once they had all their bags packed, the four of them walked back over to Mary and Jim's. Before Dial and Pepper left they watched Mary and Jim open the bag of trinkets that the four of them had been collecting for them. Mary's face lit up, she gave Dial and Pepper big hugs. More hugs went around, the last hug to be given was between Dial and Midnight. They both teared up a little bit but Dial kissed Midnight on the cheek and her and Pepper walked out the door. Not before Pepper told James to take care of his daughter, James nodded, and off Pepper and Dial were.

Chapter 6

It had only been a few hours since her parents had left to continue their journey. Midnight knew that her mother was missing her, she was missing her mother as well. Midnight however needed to focus on staying calm. Because in those few hours her baby bump went from nothing to looking like she was at least two and a half to three months along. Midnight was by no means gonna call her mother, it would only worry her.

All Midnight could feel was thirst, she drank almost a gallon of water in a short time. She drank half of a twelve pack of pop in about five to ten minutes, Midnight was still feeling dehydrated and it was only getting worse. Mary had suddenly brought her a very fresh cup of blood, after Midnight had graciously drank the cup of blood she wasn't thirsty anymore. "Well our child is definitely part vampire, but since you're human, I'm not sure how human it's gonna be", she spoke while looking at James.

James just smiled and shrugged, he didn't care how human or vampire their kid was going to turn out. Just how healthy it was going to be. Even though he was a human that got accepted into a vampire family he couldn't be happier, he was where he belonged. "James, can I talk to you for a moment?", Midnight asked with a fading smile. James looked worried but nodded, they went into another room, she looked at James and cut right to the chase.

"Are you going to leave me and my family because of us being vampires, me being pregnant, and you being human?" Midnight now looked upset. After she asked her question she put looked to the ground upset and afraid of what the answer was going to be. James put his hand under her chin and lifted her face up to look at him while he spoke, "Midnight, I knew what I signed up for when you told me that you and your family are vampires.

I'm not going anywhere", Midnight smiled and gave James a lovingly deep kiss that lasted a few minutes. After talking and being reassured, they told Jim and Mary good night and went to bed. When Midnight woke up the next morning, James wasn't in bed. She went downstairs to get some breakfast. With not being sure of how long she was going to be pregnant, she wanted to make sure that she took good care of herself.

Midnight surprised herself with how much she ate and drank for breakfast. By the time that she was full, James returned very dirty. Midnight was confused so with a confused look on her face she looked at him and asked, "Hun, why are you so dirty?, what were you doing?" James just smiled and answered, "I was out in the barn helping Jim with things". Midnight smiled and said, "oh, good, now come have some breakfast, I just finished eating".

James nodded his head, grabbed some food, and sat by Midnight. Out of the blue, Midnight asked James, "do you think mom and dad are alright?" With a mouthful, James nodded. Midnight went up to their room to call her mom anyway. She sat on the bed and slowly dialed the number, she was worried about bothering their fun. When her mother answered the phone, she could tell that her mother was a little bit drunk. Midnight smiled and said, "it sounds like you're having fun wherever you are mom".

Dial replied with, "hell yeah, we are at a bar with an equal number of men and women. There is music, obviously booze, and I'm having a blast". Midnight continued to smile and said, "I'm glad you're having fun this morning. I'm going to let you go, have fun mom, I love and miss you". Dial replied, "I love and miss you too sweetheart, talk to you later". Midnight heard a click and that phone call was ended, she sat on the bed for a moment missing them but happy her mom is happy.

She went back downstairs, Mary was working in the kitchen, Jim was still out in the barn, and James was finishing up his breakfast. Midnight decided to sit and relax in the living room, meanwhile she was starting to think about where her parents could be and where they were going. Her mother was passed out drunk in a motel room and her dad was out getting her a hangover breakfast, when he came back she was still passed out naked.

Pepper set down the food and coffee and went to sit down next to her to wake her up. He couldn't help but think as she was slowly waking up, "I really did marry the greatest most beautiful woman on earth. I am so lucky and happy with how our life has gone since the first day I laid eyes on her". While he was thinking this, he was smiling and being patient with how slow Dial was waking up. Once she had her eyes open and was smiling at him, squinting at the bright sun shining through the rusted, dusty window.

Pepper got up and gave her, her coffee first, he let her sit up against the wall near the head of the bed. Once sat up and a couple sips had been drank, and words had been said, Pepper handed her the breakfast. While handing the food to her he said, "I know it's not the most ideal breakfast in bed but it's food I know you like". After emptying her mouth and washing it down she smiled and said, "Hun, it's perfect and delicious.

I'm just hoping that one of these days I'll be able to do this for you while you recover from a hangover". Pepper just grew a huge smile on his face, kissed her forehead and went to prepare his shower. While Dial was having breakfast, Pepper was showering. He got out, got dressed and sat on the bed next to her, not in a hurry to go anywhere. Once Dial washed the last of the food down with the last of her coffee she smiled at Pepper, gave him a kiss and also went to shower.

As she was walking to the shower, Pepper was staring at her naked butt and smiling. While Dial was in the shower she had a thought, "instead of getting dressed right away, I should stand soaked and naked in the doorway". As this thought crossed her mind, she smiled very big and hurried to finish her shower. Before she did her plan, she popped her head out the door to not only make sure that Pepper was still in the room but was awake.

To her relief he was both, she opened the door wide, and with sexy slowness she put her arm up the door frame. One hand was on her hip, one of her feet were popped, her head was slightly tilted her head and had a sexy look on her face. Dial waited a moment or two for Pepper to notice her since he was on his phone, since he still hadn't noticed her she cleared her throat to let him know she was there. It worked, he looked up slightly surprised, but he grew a sexy grin on his face and said, "is that so my sexy love?"

She smiled and nodded, she slowly started walking towards him. Pepper took his tank top off, and just sat there until she got to the bed. Dial started at the end of the bed and slowly sexily started climbing up the bed towards him, this had obviously turned him on since he almost instantly got a hard-on. His shaft was started getting uncomfortable in his shorts, he took his shorts off to be more comfortable. Pepper was now in his boxers with a half way hard shaft, she smiled at what her crawling had done to her love.

Dial stopped when she was in between his legs, smiled and said, "before we get to the fun stuff, I'm gonna give you a little foreplay". She then lowered herself to the lower part of his body, pull out his already hard long shaft and put her mouth on it. When she had a gut feeling that he was about to explode in her mouth she stopped and started kissing up his upper body. Dial got up to his neck, she slightly pulled her lips away to sexily tickle and breath on his neck.

This made him even harder, all of a sudden she went from being soft to giving him a hard lustful hickie. When she was done the bruised area was bigger than she was expecting it to be, this made her smile. Pepper quickly and sexily grabbed her and was able to flip the both of them over, so he was on top. This time he started kissing her all over, making her wiggle with horniness until neither of them could take it anymore.

Dial finally started begging him to slid it into her, at first it was slow and loving. With how horny they both were, she started kissing his neck roughly which started making him go faster. Not only did he start going faster but he also started thrusting harder, making her moan loudly and happily. He slowed down to try to make their love making last longer, they went like this for a good hour or so. By the end of it they were both sweating, breath heavily, and soaking wet from each other's juices.

Once it was all done, and they both had exploded their juices, they just laid next to each other breathless. While they were trying to catch their breaths, they had huge smiles on their faces, when Dial had finally caught her breath she got up and went to the bathroom. After she was done she got dressed and sat on the bed, still not in a hurry to go anywhere. It took Pepper a little longer to catch his breath considering he was on top thrusting.

Once he did however he as well got up and went to use the bathroom, Dial stared at his naked butt as he went to the bathroom as well. Pepper came back looking less like he just had wild animal sex. He got dressed, sat on the bed next to his wife and just looked at her for a few minutes. He then asked, "so my dear, when would you like to hit the road again?" Dial looked around the room to think for a moment then answered, "I think we should go for a long walk.

Just walking everywhere, anywhere, enjoying the earth's scenery and seeing how far we can go". He looked at her a little confused but with a smile then said, "you want to go walking?, since you want to enjoy the scenery I'm guessing you don't want to use any of our vampire speed?" All Dial could do was smile and ask, "so what do you say, you want to go walking with your wife?" She held out her hand to him. Pepper, with a smile on his face as well, took her hand after grabbing a bag of snacks and walked out the door with her.

Both of them were as happy as can be, walking hand in hand down the road. All they had with them was a bag full of snacks and drinks. Seeing how sunny it was they brought probably more snacks and drinks than they needed. As they were walking however, Dial couldn't help but wonder how their daughter was doing since she first found out that she was pregnant. Dial decided to ask out loud, "do you think we should call and check up on our daughter?"

Pepper just smiled and replied, "no my dear, I think that if there's a problem, they will call us". Dial gave a slight smile back and said, "yeah, you're probably right". Pepper then kissed her on the hand and they continued walking towards the darker part of the sky. Meanwhile, Midnight and James were heading for a nap. Mary kept checking up on them every now and again, and Jim just kept working around the farm like it was any other time of day.

Midnight didn't know how tired she was, she slept the rest of the day, all night, and most of the next day. James wasn't that tired, so he was up, and Midnight was still sleeping. Every once in a while she would start to sweat pretty badly while she was sleeping, so James took a damp cold cloth and put it on her forehead. Sometimes he would just sit at her side in bed and watch her. It might seem creepy to some people but to others, it was a sign of care, and love.

When she finally woke up, she rolled over to look at her night stand. When she did, she saw a tray with fake black, blue, and red flowers (which were her favorite). There was also a nice tall glass of blood, with her favorite breakfast food which was blueberry waffles, sausage patties and scrambled eggs with ham chunks. Midnight grew a huge smile after seeing what all was there, when she went to sit up, she tried to sit up fast.

The reason she had to slow down is because in the time that she was sleeping, her belly grew faster that the average pregnant woman. Midnight wasn't in any pain, so she wasn't worried about it right now. She was just hungry, so she was just focused on was eating the food that was next to her, it had to have been made fresh because it was still very warm. After she was done eating and drinking, she got dressed, grabbed the tray, and went downstairs.

She left the flowers in the room, when she got downstairs, she didn't see anyone around, so she washed the dishes that were in her hand. When she finished washing the dishes, she just stood in the doorway and stared out into the horizon that laid beyond the farm's field and trees. The sky was a beautiful royal blue, a few clouds were in the sky, with how round they looked, it looked like there were white gumdrops in the atmosphere.

Midnight brought her eyes back towards the farm and animals, off in the distance she could see that not only was the field a beautiful emerald green, but Jim and James were out there doing field work. Mary was walking up to the house with eggs in her hands, looking like she was wearing rags. When Mary finally looked up she saw Midnight, smiled, and waved, Midnight smiled and waved back. Mary walked into the kitchen where Midnight was sitting, Midnight asked, "it was you who made me the breakfast wasn't it?"

Mary smiled and said, "I'm happy you're finally awake, no, James was the one that cooked. Got the tray ready for you and has been taking care of you while you were sleeping. How did you sleep by the way?" Midnight smiled with a little bit of shock but replied, "I slept wonderfully thank you". Mary just looked at Midnight, smiled and nodded. Midnight spoke once again, "I'll have to thank James when he comes back in, until then, would you like any help around here?"

Mary spoke while washing up the eggs, "actually, I'll let you help me, but I'd like to take an ultrasound. Seeing that your belly is bigger than it should be right now". Midnight just nodded, got up and walked into the patient room. After Mary finished up washing the eggs and putting them in the fridge, she went into the patient room with Midnight. She put the goo on her belly and started the ultrasound, she wouldn't let Midnight see anything at first because she wanted to make sure that everything was ok.

Just then, she saw the most shocking thing she'd ever seen in her life. Mary had to try and hide her expression from Midnight though, because she didn't want Midnight to start freaking out. Mary went over Midnight's belly three, four, five times just to try and make sure she wasn't seeing things. When Midnight realized that the ultrasound was taking longer than normal, she asked if everything was ok. Mary nervously giggled and said, "um, yeah, everything is perfectly fine, no need to worry". Midnight instantly started freaking out and demanded to see the screen, Mary hesitated but started turning the screen towards her very slowly. Midnight looked at the screen for a moment but for some reason couldn't really tell what she was looking at, so she asked,

"Mary, what are we looking at?" Mary hesitated to answer but said, "Midnight...........you have two heart beats in your belly. That means, you have two babies in your belly". Midnight instantly dropped her jaw in shock.

Chapter 7

At first, Midnight was speechless, Mary then piped in and said, "you sit tight, I'll run and fetch James". Midnight was unable to say anything that that moment, Mary returned about twenty minutes later with James. James rushed to Midnight's side and asked, "Hun, is everything ok? Mary said you needed me right away". At this point Midnight was able to choke out a few words such as, "I think you need to look at the screen".

Mary turned the screen towards Midnight and James, after a taking a minute to look at the screen, James instantly started smiling and looked back at Midnight. Midnight asked, "James, do you know what you are looking at?" James nodded and said, "Babe, you have two babies in your belly". Midnight smiled worriedly and nodded, James kissed her forehead and said, "after you're done in here, I want you to come into the kitchen. There is something I want to give you".

James rushed off to the kitchen and sat down anxiously. Midnight got the goo cleaned off of her, pulled her shirt back down and waddled into the kitchen. James had her sit down, as she did, he knelt on the floor in front of her with a huge smile on his face. He grabbed her hand and started speaking, "Midnight, since the first time I laid eyes on you when you and your family let me into your house from the rain, I fell in love. I couldn't have ever asked for a better partner, you're so caring, generous and I feel like you and I are both psychos.

Especially when it came to killing all those innocent people. I have been wanting to do this for a while now but never had the chance, so now that I have the chance, I'm taking it.........
Midnight, will you be my wife?" Mary, standing in the doorway just looked at said, "awe". Midnight grew a huge smile and just like every woman when getting proposed to, she started crying. She instantly said, "yes, James yes I will marry you!" she kissed him again and again.

After they were done kissing, James grew the biggest smile and said, "I'd pick you up and spin you around happily, but I don't want to hurt you or the baby. So, for now I will just give you a great big hug and lots of kisses". Midnight just smiled and replied with, "that's ok James, I'll take whatever you got". They both smiled as big as they could and gave each other lots of kisses and hugs, James then handed Midnight her phone.

He asked her, "would you like to call your parents and tell them the good news?" Midnight once again just smiled, nodded vigorously, and grabbed her phone from her fiancé. She dialed the phone as quickly as she could, before her mom could finish saying hello. Midnight bud in, "mom!, mom!, mom!, you and dad will never guess what just happened!" she finally quieted down, so her mom had a chance to speak. Dial finally spoke, "what Hun?, is everything ok?, what's going on?"

Midnight was so happy and excited that she accidently yelled into the phone, "James and I are getting married mama!". There was silence for a minute, then Dial asked, "Midnight, I don't think we heard you quite right, did you say you and James are getting married?". "Yes!", Midnight responded excitedly but a little more, quiet. Once again, there was a moment of silence, then all of a sudden her mother started screaming.

However, it didn't sound like a bad scream, more like an excited, happy scream. Once she caught her breath she said, "oh hunny, that's wonderful!" Midnight cut in, "there is one more piece of good news". Again, there was a pause, then Midnight finally said, "mom, James and I are having twins, they are both healthy". Once again, her mother started screaming again, still excited and happy screaming. Midnight started laughing, and so did her dad.

Her mom started pacing the floor excited, not sure what to do. That's when her dad finally had a chance to say something, "Midnight, James, I'm very happy for you. However, Midnight there is something I have to say to you in person". Midnight's smile quickly faded, and she asked, "dad, is everything ok?" Pepper quickly said, "yes, yes, everything is fine, what I have to say isn't bad. We will see y'all tomorrow".

Midnight just said, "ok dad, sounds good, I love you both". Her mother was still screaming, but screamed out, "I love you too". Her father said, "I love you too, goodbye". After Midnight put the phone down, she gave James a kiss, a hug, then said, "I'm gonna go take a nap dear". James just kissed and hugged her back, then nodded, he decided to go take a nap with her. Once they got to the bed, they started cuddling, James cuddled her right to sleep.

Meanwhile, back in Las Vegas, Dial was pacing the floor very excited. Pepper was sitting on the bed staring at the floor, occasionally watching Dial. He was thinking about what his daughter just told him, not only that, he was thinking about what heart filled thing he wanted to tell her. Dial was too excited to notice how quiet Pepper was, she paced for a good hour or so, when she finally got tired, she kissed Pepper on the forehead and went to bed.

Pepper was still sitting at the end of the bed, staring at the floor, thinking, contemplating, wondering. There might have been something that was bothering him, he just couldn't put his own finger on it. He didn't want to say anything to Dial, he didn't want to worry her. Pepper finally decided to lay down with his wife, regardless of weather or not he was going to fall asleep right away. Even if he was quite emotionally himself right now, that wasn't gonna stop him from laying with the most beautiful woman he had ever laid eyes on.

As they both laid there, Pepper just staring, and Dial sound asleep with a smile on her face. The one thing Pepper couldn't help but think, "how in the world did I get so lucky as to trip into this life. One minute, me and my siblings are fighting over who gets the first bite of food. The next, I'm not only a vampire and have a family, but I get to lay next to the most breath-taking woman ever". Pepper was finally able to fall asleep smiling and staring at his wife.

The next morning came, even though Pepper and James hadn't called each other, they both brought their women breakfast in bed. It took a while for the women to wake up to it, but once they did, they had a smile from ear to ear. Pepper was already dressed and ready to head out the door, Dial quickly finished her breakfast, then got dressed as fast as she could. She and Pepper rushed out the door and used their vampire speed to rush to their daughter.

After Midnight got finished she too got dressed as quickly as she could, and rushed downstairs to anxiously await her parents. It only took Dial and Pepper a few minutes to get there, once they did, lots of hugs and kisses went around. Hugs even went to Mary and Jim, who took care of both James and Midnight. They all sat down in the living room, Dial sat next to her daughter and James on the couch, Pepper sat in a chair. Mary and Jim sat across the room, Dial immediately turned to Midnight and held her hand out anxiously for her daughter's hand.

Midnight knew what her mom wanted to see, however, she didn't have a ring on her hand, not yet anyway. James quickly pulled it out of his pocket and put it on Midnight's hand, when her mother looked she saw a gorgeous black ring. The ring did not have any sparkles on it, just the way Midnight liked it. Dial's face lit up when she took a good look at the ring, just then Midnight also pulled out the ultrasound of the twins. Once again, Dial's face lit up, only this time she started crying, they were tears of pure joy.

Once Dial started crying, so did Midnight and then Mary. Seeing how happy Midnight was, made James tear up a little, but of course he wouldn't let it show. After Mary's tears subsided, she went into the kitchen to make everyone some snacks and tea. Midnight thought it was nice to not have blood for a change, and luckily so did her unborn children. Midnight had had her fill of tea and snacks, so she politely asked for a glass of animal blood, Mary just smiled and nodded.

It was silent for a few moments, Midnight then asked her parents when they were heading out again, and where they were going. Dial and Pepper just looked at each other and Pepper said, "we haven't really talked about it. We've been mostly just winging it out and about. Midnight, do you remember that there was something I wanted to talk to you about?" Midnight nodded her head, then Pepper asked Dial if him and her could trade spots.

Dial nodded her head and got up, Pepper came and sat where she was, next to their daughter. He turned to her and said, "Midnight I know that I haven't been the most talkative with what's been going on in your life. I just want you to know that I am very proud of you, of the independent woman you have become. I'm over the moon happy that you are happy, and I am very grateful to have you as my daughter. It might sound like there is a but coming, but I can assure you that there isn't.

I love you and I am once again so over the moon grateful that you are my daughter". Everyone was shocked, and Midnight was crying during and after her dad's speech, even Dial was tearing up a bit. Jim was happy that everyone was happy and joyful, but he decided to go do some farm work. James decided to go with him, while the women and the one giving the speech sit in the house being joyful and soaking up the glorious moment.

It's not that they weren't happy and excited about what was going on, they were. It was just that they both had the mentality that since they were men, they couldn't be sappy about much for too long. Otherwise they felt like they were going to be seen more feminine than they actually were. Since they didn't have much to do with the animals or cleaning the barn up, James decided to pet some of the animals and play with them a little bit.

He mostly just pet the horses, Pepper came out after a little bit. The men could tell that he hadn't been crying since his eyes weren't red. Jim went back over to where James and Pepper were, he noticed that one of the stalls hadn't been cleaned yet, which was no big deal. He then handed Pepper a pitchfork and a shovel and said, "you should know where the wheel-barrel is, there is a pen over there that needs cleaning. Before you ask, you will be paid in blood, just like when you started working here.

By the way, you just stopped working here, I was guessing that you quit since you got a family. Is that true or what happened with that situation?" Pepper just slightly smiled and said, "yeah, I guess that's what happened. To tell you the truth, I'm not really sure myself". Jim held out a hand for a hand-shake and said, "then let's make it official". Pepper nodded, held out his hand as well and said, "yes, Jim, I quit". They both smiled and slightly chuckled, but they knew that nothing was going to change just because they made it official.

James kind of chuckled too, he wasn't really eavesdropping since the three of them were standing in a circle. The men were just standing out in the barn, grooming the horses, talking about the other animals. They were also talking about seasons and field work, meanwhile, the women were back inside. They were getting rid of their tears, cleaning up to make dinner, and chatting about names and genders. Dial started off with, "so, do we know what the little ones are?".

Midnight smiled, nodded, and said, "one boy and one girl". Dial smiled again and said, "you know what would be the perfect name for a boy? Jack". Midnight took a moment to think about the name then smiled and said, "I like it, but I'd rather have a few names picked out so that James and I can decide on one later". Dial just smiled and nodded, Mary piped in and said, "I almost think that Angel would be a good name for a girl".

All three of them smiled, Midnight then said, "there now we have a list started for my kid's names". They all started giggling when she said that, both Dial and Midnight were helping Mary cook dinner. Once dinner was made, Mary grabbed the dinner triangle, walked to the front door and started ringing the crap out of it. She rang it for a good minute, as hard as she could, that way the men knew that dinner was ready, and it was their only warning.

Mary knew that it would take the men a few minutes to get up to the house, wash up, and get seated. Her and the two women got the table all ready, even got the drinking cups filled. Since Dial and Midnight already knew where their men were going to sit, they filled up their plates with what they knew the men would like and eat. The men finally made it back up to the house, went to the bathroom, took turns washing up, and went back to the kitchen.

Dial and Midnight were feeling so generous that they had the chairs pulled out waiting for their loves. They all sat down, but since Dial's family wasn't religious, they didn't pray. Mary and Jim just sort of sat quietly and awkwardly eating, they were praying in their heads. That way they wouldn't disturb Dial's family but also, so they could keep their "routine and faith" alive. Since Midnight was pregnant, she was the hungriest.

She had three or four platefuls of the feast they were having. The shocking part is that when everyone was pretty close to being done with dinner, there was still enough left to feed two or three people. They were all just sitting there, letting their stomachs settle from dinner, Mary piped in and said, "well at least we have some leftovers, ha ha". They all smiled, but since they were full, they didn't even giggle. Luckily for Dial and Pepper, Mary and Jim had yet another room for them to stay in.

Their house could comfortably fit everyone in it, they were very happy with it. Midnight got up, walked over to Mary, bent over and gave her a hug and kissed her on the forehead. She then held out her hand for James to grab, once he did she yelled, "night everyone!", and they all yelled, "night!" back. Jim leaned in, gave his wife a kiss, then went to bed. Pepper just gave her a smile, a nod, and a thank you, then headed off to bed himself.

It was just Mary and Dial left in the kitchen, Mary looked at Dial and said, "you can go to bed as well if you want Hun". Dial smiled, shook her head no, and said, "no, I'd like to stay up and help you clean up, if that's ok with you". Mary just smiled and nodded, she started by taking a couple of dirty plates from the table and taking care of them. Dial did the same, however, when they finished clearing the table of the dirty dishes, she looked at Mary and said, "tell you what, you put the food away.

Bring me the rest of the dirty dishes then go get us some beers please". Mary was going to start saying no to that but then thought about it and just smiled and nodded again. While Mary was working at the table, Dial was washing everything that needed to be washed, even if it wasn't from dinner. Mary sat down at the table after she grabbed them some beers, Dial did the same after everything was washed and put away.

After her first sip, Mary said, "thank you for helping me, even though you didn't have to". Dial swallowed her sip and responded, "you're taking care of my pregnant daughter and my soon-to-be-son-in-law. Doing the dishes and hanging out with you while having a beer is the least I could do". They clinked, finished their beers, then went to bed. Right before Dial fell asleep she said to Pepper, "I can't believe we are gonna be grandparents".

Pepper was asleep but Dial still fell asleep happy about it.

Chapter 8

Morning came, the beautiful sun was just up enough for there to be different colors in the sky still. It came as a surprise to James though, because him and Midnight had finally woken up at the same time. The best part was that they were facing each other and smiling at each other. Midnight spoke, "good morning my fiancé". James smiled bigger and said, "good morning to you my beautiful fiancé". Midnight spoke again, "you know, since we are laying here, it would be the perfect time to come up with names for our unborn children".

James just continued to smile and then asked, "what did you have in mind, my dear?" Midnight responded with, "well I've got a pretty good start to a small list, for both our daughter and our son. For our son, I was thinking either Jack or Alex. For our daughter, I was thinking either Rose or Sophie". James was just smiling away, Midnight then asked, "what do you think?" He took a moment then replied, "I almost think we should give them a Greek god and goddess name".

Midnight, also smiling away, said, "I like that idea, we can add those names to the list we already have". James nodded, they were both quiet for a few moments. James then spoke, "I'm thinking, Poseidon for a boy, and Aphrodite for a girl". Midnight was somehow able to smile even bigger and said, "Hun, I love those names". James chuckled and said, "good". Midnight spoke slightly quicker and said, "we should come up with just one or two more, then narrow it down to two for both.

That's when we will flip a quarter and decide who gets what name". Once again, James just chuckled and said, "ok". James spoke after chuckling, "how about Robert for a boy and Kartana for a girl?" Midnight smiled and said, "good, now we have a good list to pick from". "So, which two are your favorite girl and boy names?" Midnight asked slightly excited. "For our son, I like Poseidon, or Alex. For our daughter, I like Rose or Sophie", James responded after thinking a moment.

Midnight got a little more excited when she sat up and said, "my thoughts exactly". James pulled a quarter from his night stand and said, "I'll flip, you put the names to heads or tails. We can start with our daughter". "Ok, ok, heads, it's Sophie, tails, it's Rose", Midnight said slightly quickly. James flipped the quarter and it landed on heads, they then looked at each other smiling big. Midnight spoke again, "For heads, Alex, For tails, Poseidon".

Once again, James flipped the quarter, this time it landed on tails. Midnight got so excited that they now had their kid's names picked out she let out a littler holler and gave James a big hug. They could hear chuckling coming from down the hall, then they chuckled back. Meanwhile, down the hall where her parents were, they were whispering. "What do you think they are doing or talking about in there?" Dial asked.

"Hun we shouldn't be trying to interfere with our daughter's new life", Pepper replied while chuckling again. "But aren't you just a little bit curious?" Dial questioned slightly pleading. Before Pepper had the chance say anything, Dial spoke again, "I think they were talking about what they were going to name our grandkids". Pepper just smiled, but Dial broke in again, "we just have to remember that whatever they decide to name them, we will still love them just the same".

Pepper just sat quietly for a moment Dial broke in one last time, "isn't that right?" she looked a little more serious. Pepper lost a little bit of his smile then quickly said, "yes ma'am", then they both chuckled. "Do you think we should go downstairs anytime soon?" James asked. Dial laid back down from her sitting position, sighed and said, "I'm too lazy right now. However, if you bring me some clothes I'll get dressed and come downstairs with you", she gave him a pleading smile.

James just chuckled once more, got up, gave her, her clothes, sat back on the bed and waited. Dial almost took her time getting dressed but she was hungry, so she only hurried a little bit. Once dressed Pepper let her walk out of the bedroom first, she looked towards Midnight and James's room to see if the door was closed. It was wide open, so Midnight and James must have walked downstairs already. They got downstairs to see everyone at the table eating breakfast, there were two empty chairs waiting for Dial and Pepper.

Mary got up right when she saw Dial and Pepper and got them plates and silverware. Soon they were all eating breakfast, Jim, James and Pepper were getting ready to head outside to work. The women would clean up and chat, once all the dishes were done Dial instantly sat down on the couch while Midnight and Mary were still in the kitchen. She hollered to Midnight, "so Midnight, when do you want to start planning your and James's wedding!?"

She heard Midnight chuckled then came the sound of footsteps. Midnight sat in the chair with a glass of green tea, sighed and said, "well mom, I think the three of us women could start planning it as soon as we wanted. We obviously won't be having a lot of people, so it'll probably a really small wedding but that's ok". Dial smiled and nodded, Mary came, sat down and asked, "so what are us women talking about?" Dial said excitedly and happily, "my daughter's wedding", Midnight smiled.

Midnight piped in and said, "well first things first, the dress is obviously going to be black, lace, vintage, and somewhat long". "I could probably make you a dress if you wanted, it would be at no cost. The only thing I would ask you to do is for you and your family to go hunt some fresh animals. That way our farm can stop losing so many livestock, even if some of our animals are getting sick and dying". Midnight asked excitedly, "really, you would do that for me?, but you've already done so much for my family and myself".

Mary just smiled and nodded, then she pulled out a large pad of paper and an erasable pen. She then looked at midnight and asked, "so give me as detailed of a list as you can of how you want your dress to look please". Midnight smiled, nodded and started speaking, "well first I'd like the color to be as black as you can make it. I'd like a sweetheart neckline, strapless. Lots of lace, I'd like it to look vintage if that's possible.

For the length I'd like it to be knee length in the front and floor length in the back". Mary nodded, while writing her list and saying, "good, good, now, from head to toe, what accessories would you like?" Midnight answered with, "I'd like a black, pure lace veil, one that I flip over my face. I'd like my veil at least to the middle of my back, please not sparkles or gems or anything like that. However, I would like a tiara, since I know there are no black ones, I'd love it spray painted black.

I would like black leather gloves, with lace, but the finger part cut off down to the knuckles. The only thing I plan on wearing on any of my fingers would be my wedding ring. I'm not planning on wearing any sort of tights, I'll probably just wear short shorts. Now, finally, the footwear. I can't decide between black open wedges or boots, if I do wear boots they will be square toed, and the color is yet to be determined". After Midnight said that last thing, she finally took a deep breath and let it out slowly.

As Mary was finishing up writing she said, "ok now one final question for the bride alone. How do you want your bouquet?" Midnight grew a huge smile and said, "I'd like eleven real roses and one fake one". Mary looked confused and asked why, Midnight answered with, "because, I will love James until the last flower dies". Mary and Dial just tilted their heads and said, "awe". Midnight added, "I'd like royal blue and black if possible".

Mary was smiling, nodding and said, "we can absolutely make that work". Just then the guys came in from outside, they were covered in dirt, sweat and a little bit of hay. Each of them went to get a kiss from their women, they got one then got told to go shower and change. "Then you, me and Midnight can talk about cake and food for the wedding", Mary said to James. James just nodded, gave Midnight another kiss and headed to the bedroom which had a connected bathroom.

When Jim got done, he popped open a beer. Same with Pepper and James but James still sat with Mary and Midnight to discuss wedding stuff. Mary started off with, "ok, how many layers or tiers do you want? What kind of cake? How do you want the outside to look? Finally, the most important question. What do you want your cake toppers to be?" Mary looked up after putting semicolons after every question, James had the expression of just seeing a ghost.

Midnight was sitting cuddled with James, looking out the window, thinking of replies. Before answering, she looked at James and asked, "do you have any ideas for any of the questions she just asked?" Still in shock, James shook his head no. Midnight decided to start the answers by saying, "James at any time, I hope you know it's ok to give input on your opinions". James nodded and Midnight continued, "I think a two-tiered cake will do fine, the top tier can be one layer and the bottom can be two.

The very first layer on the bottom can be Marble, the next layer up can be chocolate. The final layer which is the top tier can be red velvet. The outside can be chocolate with spiders, spider webs, anything spooky like skulls. Anything creepy or just death-like and vampire. Midnight paused to see how James was doing, he was just sitting there still slightly shocked, but he was nodding. Midnight also rested for a minute to let Mary catch up, Mary looked up as soon as she was ready for more information.

Midnight went on to say, "I'd like "dirt" which could be

chunks of brownie or cookie. In this "dirt" at the bottom of the cake, I would like gummy worms. Now for the toppers, I can't decide if I want an edible cat-woman or vampire". Once again, she stopped to look at James who was still just smiling and nodding. Midnight nudged him gently and asked him what he wanted, she asked because she knew he hadn't been paying attention.

She also told him that he could have anything he wanted, the people making the cake would probably just make it edible. James quit nodding, thought for a minute then said, "we should have king and queen vampires". Midnight smiled and James continued, "since you're my girl, my vampire should have one hand on his hip and the other around hers. His face can be smiling and slightly blushing. For her vampire, one hand can be on his back, the other on his chest.

She can also be kissing his face". This time it was Midnight and Mary that had shocked expressions. "Her hair could be black, long and a little wavy", Midnight quickly added in. Mary happily wrote all of this down and then went and got herself a wine cooler. She came back, sat down, looked at her list and started thinking of where she was going to start first. Mary knew that she had her work cut out for herself, and the only thing she had to do was call people.

Midnight couldn't explain how she knew that alcohol would not affect her baby, she just knew. So, she as well got up and got a drink, however, when she started drinking, she felt nauseous and knew that the baby didn't like it, so she stopped immediately. She started having some cookies when all of a sudden, she was having really bad back and belly pain. Mary instantly put down her drink and her and Midnight went to the patience room.

Luckily it was baby growing faster than other babies, when Mary saw this, she was able to do a huge sigh of relief. In turn, that made Midnight relieved. They came out of the room with smiles on their faces, Midnight then gave the satisfying news that it was just the baby growing. Everyone, except for Midnight, continued to drink and relax. Once Dial got drunk and tired enough, she headed to bed, same with Pepper.

Before Jim got mean from drinking, he went to bed as well. Mary decided to start baking, first she baked a pie, then cookies. She also baked cupcakes, all of this took her until about one o'clock in the morning. Midnight had gone to bed after taking a couple cookies, Mary finally got the last batch of cupcakes cooling and the last bit of dishes done then she went to bed as well. The next morning, Midnight was the first one up, she decided to go have a cup of coffee.

Mary was awake next, she too had coffee. After their coffee, since it was still just those two awake, Mary decided to check her over. Luckily she did, because Mary discovered that Midnight's water could break at any moment. They didn't have to worry about going to wake anyone up, because the screaming and crying from Midnight from labor would wake them up. Soon enough, one by one, everyone was awake and having coffee.

After coffee, Midnight decided to make a big breakfast for everyone. She made different types of eggs, toast, bacon, and sausages. However, she was thinking about making French toast as well. Since the house was clean, there wasn't much for the women to do. They were all just waiting for Midnight's water to break. The guys, however, went outside to mess around with old vehicles, the animals, and since they had four wheelers, ride them.

Just as it was starting to get late, Midnight's water finally broke. Since she was going to be delivering right there at the house, there was no need for anyone to rush or panic at that moment. Although, when Midnight got on the patience bed, it did not take long for her to dilate. Luckily for Midnight, because of the quick dilation, she did not have much pain with her contractions. The pain did come with labor, like all labors.

Once she started pushing, she started screaming for James. Even though she was a vampire, she still felt the same pain as a human woman would. No one, not even Midnight cared that when James came running in, he was once again covered in dirt. He stood at her side regardless and let her squeeze his hand as hard as she needed to. She squeezed, screamed and pushed, all as hard as she could. Finally, there was two screaming, crying, perfectly healthy babies.

The moment Midnight and James started holding their kids after James cut both the umbilical cords, Midnight started crying at the fact of how beautiful their newborn kids were. While Midnight and James were bonding with their new kids, Mary cleaned up and got Midnight ice chips. When Midnight was ready for some rest, Mary and Dial gladly brought the new babies, Poseidon and Sophie into the other room and James went with them.

Dial didn't have social media because she couldn't risk anyone finding out that she turned into a vampire. Though she was pretty sure that no one cared, she loved taking pictures with her new grandbabies anyway. Jim and Pepper didn't come in right away with James, but when they did get inside Pepper went over to Dial and Mary to see his new grandbabies. He decided that he had to get a picture with Dial, Sophie and Poseidon.

When he was getting the pictures, Mary handed Poseidon to Pepper and went into the kitchen. Since it wasn't his family, Jim decided to sit in the kitchen with Mary. A few hours later Midnight woke up, asked for food then she was going to try to breastfeed her kids, obviously one at a time unless the other one started crying right away. James ate in the patient room with herd, after they were done, he brought their babies in the room to see if they were hungry, they both were.

Chapter 9

The only thing that James or Midnight cared about was being in that moment with their kids. Meanwhile Dial and Pepper went to bed, so did Jim but Mary stayed up and had some cookies until Midnight and James decided they were ready for bed so she could get a bed set up for James to sleep in the room with Midnight and the babies. She didn't want Midnight going up the stairs for bed since she just gave birth. It'd been at least another hour before they were ready, but when they were, Mary got them set up and went to bed herself.

That first night with their kids was pretty calm and quiet, Poseidon and Sophie didn't cry much the first night, just making noises. James kept getting up to see if Sophie and Poseidon were ok, Midnight wasn't too worried and wasn't going to be unless the babies started crying. The next morning it was just coffee and breakfast, Midnight got up and walked around for a little bit to get her body used to walking around without being pregnant again.

For and hour or so Poseidon and Sophie were still sleeping, they woke up hungry obviously. Midnight fed them at the same time until they wouldn't drink anymore, then she switched nipples once again until they wouldn't drink anymore. Dial was still trying to let the fact that she was a grandma now, sink in. She was happy that her family grew though, so was Pepper. After breakfast Pepper wanted to walk and talk with Dial, he didn't ask her in an alarming way, so she wasn't worried.

As they were walking in the warm glow of the sunrise, Pepper spoke, "would you want to go back to exploring the world with me now that our grandkids have been born?" Without hesitation Dial smiled and replied, "since I know that our daughter and grandbabies are in good care and will be safe, I would love to. We just need to make sure that when our daughter sets her wedding date, that we are back in time". This made Pepper smile and so he went to pack a couple things and some money.

Dial went to help and suggested, "we can use our vampire speed to get to the hotel in Florida. Then we can have fun for a couple days then fly somewhere, what do you think?" Pepper just smiled and responded with, "I think that sounds like a wonderful my love". As they were packing, James helped Midnight go slowly up the stairs. The got up the stairs and went to the bedroom where her parents had been staying. Once Midnight had seen what they were doing, she hugged her mom.

She then said, "please remember to send postcards from wherever you stay for a couple days or more". When the hug broke, Dial was slightly tearing up but nodded and said, "we will hunny, we will also be sure to make it back when you set a date for your wedding". Pepper had finished packing the two of them and they all headed downstairs. Jim and Mary looked slightly confused, Mary asked, "so, where y'all going this time?" Dial replied with, "I think we will go to Florida first.

Then I think we might fly somewhere". Mary just smiled and said, "that sounds like a really nice vacation". Everyone just smiled and nodded in agreement. Once the few bags that they had packed were by the door, they said their goodbyes, shed a few tears and left. It was pretty quiet after they left, all except the newborns of course. Sophie cried and screamed when she was hungry and when she needed a clean butt, just like all babies, she even cried when she wanted to sleep.

Because of all the crying that his sister was doing, this made Poseidon cry for all those things as well. However, since they were half human and half vampire, they both grew half as fast as normal human babies. How long it took human babies to grow in a month, it took Poseidon and Sophie two weeks less to grow the same amount. By the time Dial and Pepper finally got around to sending their first post card from Florida, Poseidon and Sophie were already two months old.

Not only were they two months old, they were already crawling around and starting to roll over. On one of the postcards, Dial managed to let them know how long they were staying so that they could get pictures of Poseidon and Sophie. When Midnight received the postcard, she couldn't help but smile because not only could she now send pictures, but she could now tell her parents when the wedding was going to take place.

It was going to take place in a couple months, right there at the farm. That's what Midnight, James, and Mary had decided, Jim couldn't care either way. Jim was just happy that he didn't have to be the one to make any decisions, he was just going to show up as a guest. He was also going to be on the property because it was his and he lived there, but he still didn't care if the wedding took place there. Even though Mary already knew where she was going to have the wedding take place, it was the last thing she decided to get set up for the wedding.

Things like the dress, the cake and other details that were minor and major got decided first. Although Mary knew where the wedding was going to be, she still needed to figure out what part of the farm it was going to be on. She also needed to figure out what kind of aisle there was going to be, what Midnight, James, and the solemniser were going to stand under for the wedding. Midnight told Mary to let her know when she had the placement mostly figured out so she and James could pick a date, that way she could let her mom know when the date was.

That way it could give Dial and Pepper enough time to pack what they wanted to get packed and head back home. It was about roughly a month before the wedding, Dial and Pepper made it back, while Mary was working on getting the ceremony set up Dial was helping Midnight take care of the kids. At this point in time the kids were almost a year each, so they were a little easier to take care of than newborns. Also, they were both physically and mentally a little older than a year, Dial enjoyed her time with her grandkids anyway.

Jim, James, and Pepper were just in and out of the house doing guy stuff and helping the women whenever they needed it. It was about half way through the month, everything was looking wonderful for the wedding. The dress fit Midnight perfectly, it was gorgeous, James was just going to wear an outfit of nice bootcut blue jeans. He was also going to wear a white, long-sleeve button-up, a black vest, a black Stetson cowboy hat.

Last but not least, the boots, a pair of square toed black cowboy boots with silver spurs. Everything fit everyone perfectly, Poseidon and Sophie were able to walk very decently by now, so they were going to be the flower girl and the ring bearer. Pepper and Jim were going to be James's best-man and groomsman, Dial and Mary were going to be Midnight's maid-of-honor and bridesmaid. The men wore something similar to what James was wearing, the women wore sweet-heart neckline, strapless, long navy-blue dresses.

Poseidon was going to wear a nice navy-blue long-sleeve button up with bootcut blue jeans, Sophie was going to wear nice bootcut blue jeans with a long-sleeve navy-blue plain shirt. Both the kids were going to be wearing cowboy and cowgirl hats with little black boots, Mary wanted everyone to get dressed to make sure that everything was going to fit everyone and make them look good. Not only did everything fit but even the kids looked so good that Dial, Midnight and Mary all tilted theirs heads and said, "awe".

After final checks of fitting and how everything looked, everyone went back to their relaxing clothes and just sat around, it was getting pretty late anyway. Since the present day was a Saturday, and the pastor wasn't going to be in until the following day, everyone took this opportunity to just relax the whole day. Everyone except Dial and Midnight were able to relax the whole day, they had the important job of watching and taking care of the kids.

Since it was a beautiful day, they were able to go outside and play, they just made sure to stay away from the area where the wedding was going to take place. The area of where the wedding was going to take place was actually slightly small, they had the rest of the farm to play on and around. The farm was pretty big, so they had a lot of room, this made the kids happy and smile and in turn made Dial and Midnight happy.

Poseidon and Sophie knew they were going to have the best day when not only was the hay-loft was free to play on but it was also full of hay bales to play on. However, since the kids weren't big enough to play unsupervised, if they wanted to climb the hay bales all the way to the top, Dial and Midnight were going to have to climb with them. They didn't mind though because it gave Dial and Midnight the chance to be somewhat kids and just have fun in the hay.

Just as they knew, Midnight and Dial ended up having to follow the kids up, up, up. Once they all got to the top, Midnight and Dial decided to suggest making a fort out of the hay bales. The kids loved the idea but didn't know how, so since Dial had more experience with this than Midnight did, she decided to show all three how to. Midnight finally popped in and helped when Dial had the bases of where the "kitchen" and "living room" were.

Midnight made and pointed to one of the "chairs" that were in the make-believe living room, using the rest of their imagination, the kids immediately jumped in and helped. Sophie pointed to one, asked for it to be moved to a certain spot, and said, "this could be a pillow for one of the "beds"". This made both Midnight and Dial smile, and since Midnight was just slightly stronger, since she just had kids, she was the one who moved the bale over to where Sophie had pointed.

Poseidon got excited and started shouting, "my turn, my turn!" he was able to drag one hail bale at a time to where he imagined another bed would be. The four of them kept playing like this all day for hours, since they didn't have a clock or phone to look at because they left all electronics inside, someone had to come out and tell them when it was lunch time and also when it was dinner time. They didn't even give their stomachs time to digest any food, they started climbing while they were still chewing their mouthfuls.

However, after dinner time, they weren't able to stay out much longer because of how dark and late it was getting. Even though there was a light post out by the bales, it was still dark to the point where Dial and Midnight said that it was time to head inside for the night. Because of the fact that Poseidon and Sophie got to play all day, not only were they ok with going in, but they were also getting tired. Unlike most nights, that night it was pretty easy for Midnight to get her kids to bed.

It was easier because of all the energy they used to play on and around the bales. After Midnight got the kids in bed however, she decided to crack open a beer, a Coors light to be exact. Her mom wasn't quite tired yet though, so she decided to stay up with her daughter, chat and have a beer as well. When Dial got sat down with her beer, she took a sip, looked at her daughter, paused for a second then started asking her questions.

Questions like, "are you getting cold feet at all?" Right away Midnight looked confused and replied with, "no, why would I be getting cold feet?" Dial instantly responded with, "it's perfectly natural to get cold feet when it gets closer to the commitment, almost every woman goes through it". Midnight took another sip and said, "no, I'm very excited to be marrying James, he makes me happy, he loves our kids and is a great dad.

Plus, he doesn't hate my parents which is another plus". Her response made Dial chuckle a little, then her next question was, "even though Mary put together your wedding from the answers you were giving her. When she was asking you all those questions about the wedding, and you were giving her answers. That was a long time ago now, even though the wedding it just around the corner, are you happy with how everything is turning out so far?"

This made Midnight pause for a minute and think about her mother's detailed question, she then took another sip, started nodding her head and said, "you know what mom, yeah I am happy with how things are turning out. With the wedding, with my family, with everything. I am very happy that not only was Mary able to get my answers on paper, but also execute them better than I could have ever imagined".

The only thing that Dial could do to her daughter's response was smile and sip some more of her beer. She sat there for a little longer thinking if she had anymore questions for her daughter since they were having deep conversations while having some beers. Dial couldn't think of any, but Midnight could, her question was, "mom, after the wedding, when James and I decide where to go for our honeymoon and how long we are going to be gone.

Would you and dad be willing to stay for that amount of time and watch your grandkids? After James and I got back, you and dad could go back to your adventures". Dial smiled and started giggling and said, "hunny, I know that your father and I would absolutely love to watch our grandkids for how ever long you and James want to be away on your honeymoon". This gave Midnight one of the biggest smiles she's had in a very long time, she then put down her last beer for the night and gave her mom the biggest hug she could.

Chapter 10

Midnight's hug made Dial giggle a little, once the hug and the giggles and the beer drinking were all done, they decided to finally go to bed since it was past midnight. Everyone else had already made it to bed, and luckily Midnight didn't wake up her kids, so she was able to slip into bed with James. It was now Sunday, Mary decided to wait for an hour after she knew that mass was over to call the pastor. When Mary got around to calling, the pastor had just sat down from finishing chatting with people after mass.

The best part of when Mary called was that the pastor didn't sound exhausted, he just listened to what Mary had to say/ask. After the hellos and the how are you questions, she asked, "would you be up for marrying a couple who is ready to be married?" The pastor's instantly reply was, "I would absolutely love to do that, would y'all need me today?" Mary said, "no but would tomorrow or sometime this week work?"

The pastor replied with, "Tuesday would work the best for me, that way I could relax the rest of today and have tomorrow to prepare". All Mary could say to that was, "sounds good to me father, we will see you on Tuesday then". Once they agreed, they said their goodbyes and hung up the phone, Mary had a huge smile on her face and did a little happy dance. Now that Mary got the very last detail setup, she knew that they could all have the rest of the day and the next day to relax.

She made sure to tell the bride and groom however when the pastor was going to make it there. Midnight knew that the pastor was the final detail, so she was looking even more forward to her wedding, she was so thankful to Mary for setting everything up and getting everything ready. Midnight wasn't sure if she was going to ever be able to pay her back or do something that was as equally as amazing as Mary was. Today was a little different than yesterday, Midnight stayed inside, while her parents went and played with her kids.

From the moment that they started playing in the hay bales, the four of them were having so much fun that they lost track of time and someone had to go out and let them know that it was lunch and dinner time. Since her kids and parents were occupied, Midnight took almost the whole day to sleep as much as she could to get rested and ready for the following day, her wedding day. Meanwhile, Mary was walking around in the ceremony area to make sure everything was perfect.

James and Jim decided to mess around with some of the old vehicles, they were next to the hay loft. Everyone except Midnight was outside, Pepper, Dial, Sophie and Poseidon were still in the hay loft having fun. Jim and James were still messing around with old vehicles, Mary was finishing up with the ceremony area. When Mary was done, even though her place was in the house and taking care of women things, she decided to go see if she could be any help to the guys and the vehicles.

Now everyone was not only outside but they were roughly all in the same area, when Mary couldn't be of any help, she decided to watch Dial, Pepper, Sophie and Poseidon play in the loft. When Midnight woke up, she realized that everyone was outside playing and messing around. She decided that since it was a hot enough day, she would make some sun tea and bring out multiple glasses on a tray. The first person to see her bringing out the tea was her soon-to-be husband.

James immediately stopped what he was doing, grew a huge smile on his face and started walking over to her. Jim had asked James for a certain tool, when Jim hadn't received it, he looked behind him to see if James was still there. He saw that James had disappeared, looked around for a minute for him and saw that he was having a refreshing glass of tea that Midnight brought out. Jim thought having a refreshment was a good idea, so he stopped what he was doing as well, walked over to where the tea was and had a glass himself.

Soon enough everyone was having tea, it was hot enough, and they were needing energy anyway. Even Midnight, who brought it out, was having a glass. Once everyone had a glass and was drinking, Midnight decided to put the tea on a table just outside the house, that way the tea could get stronger. When everyone was done with their glasses and had enough, they brought their glasses to Midnight and went back to what they were doing.

All except Mary who decided to help Midnight bring them in and wash them. Also, since it was a beautiful day, and there were no little to no bugs to be seen, Midnight and Mary decided to open a couple of windows and open the front door. It was nice to be able to let some fresh air in, especially after a long winter of "hibernation". The tea was so good, that everyone including the kids wanted more, so everyone went and got another glass.

Not only that, they were drinking it outside, the longer the tea stayed in the sun, the stronger it got. Midnight just kept making sure that there was plenty of ice in the tea jar, because of how hot the sun was, it would have made the tea warm. If the tea got too warm, it would have lost some of its irresistibleness. The kids were wanting to get new cups each time they wanted some tea, Midnight told them, "you can reuse the same sippy cups that you grabbed.

You don't have to keep getting clean ones, we can just wash your cups when you think that you have had all the fill of tea that you want. Also, if you want something other than tea to drink, we can just rinse the cup out and put the new beverage in it. Do you understand?" Both Poseidon and Sophie nodded their heads and put the new clean sippy cups back where they grabbed it from. They then grabbed their cups that had the tea in it, handed them to their mother and asked for more tea.

Midnight happily nodded her head, took the cups, filled them up, and gave them back to her kids. James and Dial were just leaning against the door-way, watching Midnight parent her kids, they couldn't help but smile. They smiled because not only, did Midnight teach her kids something, but she looked like a natural mom teaching them. Midnight looked up, saw her fiancé and mom watching her, and she asked, "what's up guys?"

Dial instantly replied with, "we were just watching you be a wonderful mother to two beautiful kids, teaching them that they don't have to get a new cup each time they want some of the same beverage. It was a very beautiful moment". Her mother saying this made her blush, and the fact that her fiancé was agreeing with what her mother said, made her blush a little harder. Midnight blushing made James blush a little bit, and both Midnight and Dial thought that, that was very cute.

Midnight gave her mother the "I would like to talk to James alone" look. Dial looked at the kids and said, "ok kids, if your content with your sippy cups, you can bring them outside, let's go outside and play some more". As they were walking out the door, Dial looked up at her daughter and smiled, Midnight smiled back and nodded because she knew her mother could tell what she was wanting. Once the three of them were outside, James started following them, but Midnight said, "hey James, wait up".

That made James stop in his tracks, turn around, and ask, "yeah, what's up Hun". Midnight got comfy standing at the counter and asked, "so, are you ready to be my husband starting tomorrow?" James decided to slowly and sexily walk up to Midnight while responding with, "I am so very ready, to have this fine ass vampire be my wife for all eternity". As he was saying this, not only had he walked up to her, but he also put his hands on her hips and started sexily breathing on her neck.

He knew that this was a major turn on for her, she couldn't resist but to start breathing heavily. Once she realized that she was breathing heavily however, she slowly stepped away from him giggling because she was starting to get horny. She told him, "James, you realize that everyone is right outside, right?" James just nodded, put a sexy smile on, started walking towards her again and replied with, "yeah, I know there outside, that's the best part because they're out there and we are in here".

This made Midnight blush again and she smiled, she noticed that James was still walking towards her, so she said, "if you come any closer or try anything sexy, we are going to the bedroom, right now". James smiled, said, "good", and started breathing and kissing on her neck again. Midnight instantly grabbed his hand and started walking them to the bedroom. Once they got there, she shut the door behind her, leaned against it, grabbed James's hips, pulled him close and started making out with him.

Once they started making out and touching sexually, one touch after another made them both more and more horny. To the point where they started ripping off each-others clothing, once the clothes were all off, James put Midnight on the bed. Slowly and very passionately they began to have sex, luckily for them everyone was going to be outside for a couple of hours yet, so they could take their time. As they finished, they laid in bed, cuddling and naked with huge smiles on their faces.

Midnight spoke, "you know, I am very happy that we are not like a normal human couple. Because a normal human couple would be worried about the groom seeing the bride the night before the wedding". James just chuckled and said, "I think that might be for Christians, but I am very happy we are who we are". They both just smiled, nodded and giggled, Midnight gave James a tight hug before getting out of bed and getting dressed.

When she got out of bed she said, "my mom asked me if I was getting cold feet, I told her no, I am very excited and very ready to be yours for the rest of eternity". James just smiled and said, "that's good because I am ready to be yours as well". Midnight just smiled, the two of them finished getting dressed and went downstairs. When they got downstairs everyone was inside, Midnight went and kissed both of her kids on the head, they were at the table eating dinner.

Mary decided to make something very simple for dinner since the next night they were going to be having a huge feast. They were having macaroni and cheese and hot dogs that night. The next night they were going to be having ham, mashed potatoes, beef gravy, green bean casserole, hot rolls, corn, and salad. Everyone was looking forward to the next nights dinner, it was like a thanksgiving dinner, but for a wedding.

Everyone was done eating, it was too late to go back outside. Everyone got baths and went to bed. However, Midnight was so excited that she couldn't sleep, she decided to walk around outside since it wasn't too cold. She was the only one awake for hours just wishing that the time would speed up just a little bit, she was ready to be not only a mother but a wife as well. Even though it was dark out, there was a street light near the area of where the ceremony was going to be.

She decided to take a walk and a look around at what Mary had gotten ready for the big day. She was very impressed with what she was able to see, she was finally starting to get tired. Finally, she went back inside and was able to go back to bed without waking anyone up. The following morning, James was awake before she was, he had a feeling he knew when she was going to wake up. He brought her a cup of coffee, set it on her bedside table, and went downstairs to get some breakfast.

By the time that she woke up and was ready to have her first sip of coffee, it was cooled down enough to where it wouldn't be too hot to drink. For most people, when that first sip of coffee in the morning touches the soul. Not only does it help wake the person up, but it also warms them inside. It's like taking a really relaxing shower, it helps you get ready for the day. That day was more important than most, it was her and James's wedding day.

A day that not only was the start of the rest of their lives but a day that officially marked them as family. First, she got dressed into relaxing house clothes, just for a little while. When the priest arrived is when Midnight was going to get changed into her wedding dress, but before she would get into her dress, she would help her kids into their outfits. The priest told Mary that he would call right before he left the church, he hadn't called yet it was still pretty early.

Everyone was just finishing breakfast and cleaning up when the phone finally rang. Luckily it was the priest calling to tell Mary that he would be on his way shortly. She was so happy and excited that it was almost impossible to contain her screeching until after the phone call was over. The minute that the phone call was ended she started screaming, and everyone got scared and was scrambling to ask Mary if everything was ok.

She started giggling and nodding her head, she said, "yes, everything is wonderful, the priest will be here soon. Everything is looking wonderful for the wedding and the wedding will be starting shortly after the priest arrives!" She started screeching and jumping up and down, Jim had never seen her this excited or happy before, but he was happy to be witnessing it. At last, the priest had arrived, once again, Mary started getting very excited, she rushed herself, Dial, Midnight and the kids into the room with all their outfits.

She also knew that it would take the priest a little bit of time to get ready, so she wasn't rushing the others too bad. Since Midnight's outfit was the most important that was the last outfit to go on. Midnight made sure to tell her kids that with the clothes they were wearing, they were not to go out and play until after the part where mom and dad walk down the aisle together. Both Poseidon and Sophie understood, so they nodded their heads.

First the kids were dressed, then Dial, after her it was Mary, last but not least it was Midnight's turn to get dressed. Her mother was too emotional to help her, so Mary had Dial leave the room until her and Midnight were finished with dressing Midnight. After Midnight was completely ready, she let Dial back into the room, she started crying the minute she laid eyes on her breathtaking daughter. Because the kids were so young, they had to run through what they were all going to do.

The priest just waited patiently until the music was playing and they all were ready. Once the kids knew exactly what they had to do, Mary pushed the play button on the CD player which played the song that Midnight wanted to walk down the aisle to. Everyone got down the aisle just in time for the song to end, the wedding was going perfectly so far. The priest performed the ceremony and Dial was crying just like any mother watching her daughter get married would.

The kids were allowed to go play tag after the rings were

given and their part was done. Everyone was happy and having a wonderful time, the wedding went beautifully, and the reception was delicious. The wedding got over and everyone crashed for the night.

Chapter 11

Early the next morning, James got up first so that he could start packing his and Midnight's bags for their honeymoon. Midnight and James decided that they were just going to use the vehicle they rode in for the beginning of all their adventures together. James got the car packed and since Midnight wanted to, they waited until the kids were awake so they could say goodbye to everyone. The kids were sad that their parents were going away but they were happy about being able to spend time with their grandparents.

They hadn't seen their grandparents very often since they were always on the road, luckily, they were able take time to get to know them. That made everyone happy, when Midnight and her new husband were ready to go. They have decided that they were going to Hawaii for half of a month, not only that, they were going to fly there. Once the goodbyes were all said and the hugs were all given, they headed off to the airport.

Even though they were parents and they were already missing their kids, they decided that they were just going to enjoy their honeymoon. They got to the airport, bought their tickets, went to their flight gate, and waited until their plane was ready to board and leave. The flight attendant walked into the waiting area, clicked a button by the microphone and announced that the plane was ready to board. Midnight and James were able to be first, to hand in their tickets and get to their designated seats.

They were sat and ready to go, they were both pretty excited, Midnight was just a little bit more excited than James though. The plane filled up and the pilot announced that they were going to be taking off soon. The fasten your seatbelt sign started flashing for all the passengers to see, Midnight started freaking out a little bit after they got buckled. Even though James was freaking out as well, he decided to be as calm as he could for his new wife.

No one could tell what so ever that he was freaking out, he just held Midnight's hand until the plane was completely in the air and they were able to move if they wanted. After that, James had to go throw up because of how bad he was freaking out and making himself keep calm. He felt better, sat back down, got some water, looked at his sleeping wife, and fell asleep himself. They woke up when the fasten seatbelt sign was flashing because they would be landing soon.

Landing was a bit rough, but James just calmly held his wife's hand and when the sign was off, they unbuckled and got off the plane as fast as possible. The collected their bags, got into a taxi, rode to a nice hotel and got their room which looked like a hut from the ocean's view. They were so mesmerized by the scenery that neither of them even thought about calling Midnight's parents to see how their kids were doing.

It was their honeymoon after all, so it was understandable, they put their bags at the end of the bed. They went and stood so they could see the ocean and even touch it if they chose to. Even though they were in a hotel, they felt like they had all the privacy in the world. They could walk around naked if they wanted to, but they never did. Someone from the hotel management was a friend of Mary's and knew that Midnight and James were coming so they arranged for a giant fruit basket with a note to be put on the counter.

Someone also made sure that Midnight and James got set up with a room that had a room service button right next to the bed. It was around dinner time, there was a café menu on the bedside table that they could order dinner from. They took a look and since management was a friend of Mary's everything was already paid for, so they ordered what they wanted plus dessert and salad bar. After dinner they had half of their fruit basket and decided to watch a movie.

During the movie, James looked over at Midnight and started smiling and staring at her. She was so into the movie that she hadn't even noticed, until James started kissing on her and touching her sweetly. Since there was no one they needed to be discreet for, she not only let it happen, but she got up and sat on his lap facing him. They were still in their romantic embrace when the movie ended, neither of them stopped to turn it off so it turned itself off and they kept going.

Midnight was very happy to wake up naked, cuddling with her new husband and completely alone with him. Even though they were only going to be there for two weeks, they didn't really want to go out and do anything or see anything. They just wanted to be in each-others company, however after the third day cabin fever started kicking in. They asked the front desk where a popular place was or a market place where they could walk around.

Since everyone who worked there knew not only what room they were in but treat them like they were the most important guests, someone got them a taxi and told the taxi-man where to go. After walking around for a bit, they bought a couple souvenirs and went to the spot where they were supposed to meet the taxi-man. Even though it was a little bit of a walk, it was a beautiful day. They paid the man the amount that it would take to get them back to the hotel, sent the taxi-man on his way and walked back to the hotel.

They loved the walk, they saw some interesting people, and tried some interesting food. Some stranger on a bike with a tiny space for two people on the back, offered Midnight and James a ride for free, they said, "no thank you, we are enjoying the walk". The biker waved them goodbye and took off, Midnight and James were smiling, and they were almost as happy as can be. The only problem was that they were missing their kids and were used to being in a full house.

When they got back to the hotel, they didn't go back to their room right away, instead they continued to walk around for a bit. There was about two or three days left of their honeymoon. They were enjoying their time, but they were looking forward to getting home to their kids. Before they went home, they wanted to make sure that they went to the beach at least once. Midnight didn't care if she got a tan, she just wanted a chance to get out onto the beach and lay in her bikini.

James wanted the chance to rub sun screen on his wife on the beach since there wasn't, any nice beaches back home. Not only a chance to be in the sun and even though they had their own private beach right outside their hotel room, they were enjoying the public beach. Also, they now were able to say that they got to swim in the ocean, not just a lake. When they stepped their first foot into the ocean, it was the north pacific-ocean, it didn't feel much different than stepping into a lake back home.

They were splashing around, and swimming, hugging in the water, and throwing each other around in the water. They had their fun, packed up their stuff and went back to their hotel room to pack their bags for the next day. The following day was their last day, they could still go do and see things, but they had to be at the airport by a certain time. Midnight decided that they were going to tip the hotel for being so wonderful to them, also they had lunch before going to the airport.

They got to the airport, boarded their plane and went home. It was going to end up being around noon when they got home from their flight. Since Poseidon and Sophie knew what day their mom and dad were coming back, they waited outside all day for them. Both of their eyes lit up when they seen their parents car coming down the driveway. To make sure they wouldn't get yelled at, they stayed right where they were until they saw that the car was stopped.

No sooner than Midnight got her door closed, she was getting plowed over by her kids who missed her very much. After they were done hugging and smothering their mother with love, they raced around to the other side of the car to their dad doing the same thing they did to their mom. Once all their hugging was done, they were cute trying to help their parents inside. All the luggage was inside, the hugs were given, the pictures were shown, and dinner was now being made.

Mary decided to make a welcome home dinner for them. Grilled hamburgers and hot dogs, coleslaw, potato salad, chips and a couple other pieces of food. After dinner, Jim got a nice bonfire going so they could sit around it and Midnight and James could tell them all about their trip, they all went to bed shortly after. The following morning, Dial and Pepper decided in bed that they were going to go on more adventures, maybe go to another country.

Not only that, they loved the adventure life, they loved it so much that even though they had vampire speed, they bought a motorcycle. They knew that they couldn't take the motorcycle with them when they went to another country, but they were able to ride it all over their country. They finally came downstairs and as a surprise to everyone they were the last ones to come down for breakfast. When they came down however, they brought their bags with.

Everyone knew what that meant so no one got upset, instead after breakfast, once again, everyone said their goodbyes and walked them out the door. It was about two months later, when Midnight got a call from a strange number. She didn't answer numbers she didn't know so the number left a message, a message saying that her parents Dial, and Pepper had been in a really bad accident over in California. As soon as Midnight heard this, her face went blank, tears started falling and she dropped the phone.

James saw this so he picked up the phone, told the number

that he was Midnight's husband and asked what they had just told her. They informed him the same thing, he thanked them for the information, told them they would be on their way and hung up the phone. James put the phone down, almost ready to cry himself, but instead he looked at Midnight and before he could get another word out, she looked at him and said, "we all need to go, now".

Printed in the United States
By Bookmasters